WEST VANCOUVER MEMORIAL LIBRARY

25.97

P9-CKV-799

Withdrawn from Collection

The Mark
of the Pasha

A Mamur Zapt Mystery

Books by Michael Pearce

The Mamur Zapt Series
The Mamur Zapt and the Return of the Carpet
The Night of the Dog
The Donkey-Vous
The Men Behind
The Girl in the Nile
The Spoils of Egypt
The Camel of Destruction
The Snake-Catcher's Daughter:
The Mingrelian Conspiracy
The Fig Tree Murder
The Last Cut
Death of an Effendi
A Cold Touch of Ice
The Face in the Cemetery
The Point in the Market
The Mark of the Pasha

Sandor Seymour Mysteries
A Dead Man in Athens
A Dead Man in Tangier
A Dead Man in Trieste
A Dead Man in Istanbul

Dimitri and the One-Legged Lady

WEST VANCOUVER MEMORIAL LIBRARY

The Mark of the Pasha

A Mamur Zapt Mystery

Michael Pearce

Poisoned Pen Press

Copyright © 2008 by Michael Pearce
First Edition 2008

10 9 8 7 6 5 4 3 2 1

Library of Congress Catalog Card Number: 2007940710

ISBN: 978-1-59058-444-6 Hardcover

All rights reserved. No part of this publication may be reproduced, stored
in, or introduced into a retrieval system, or transmitted in any form, or by
any means (electronic, mechanical, photocopying, recording, or otherwise)
without the prior written permission of both the copyright owner and the
publisher of this book.

Poisoned Pen Press
6962 E. First Ave., Ste. 103
Scottsdale, AZ 85251
www.poisonedpenpress.com
info@poisonedpenpress.com

Printed in the United States of America

Chapter One

'You can have a car,' said Willoughby generously.

'Really?'

'Yes. And you can keep it afterwards for a week or two. For your personal use.'

'Gosh!'

'Well, why not? The Ministers have each got one now, Garvin's got one. Why shouldn't the Mamur Zapt have one?'

Why not, indeed?

'You should do justice to yourself, Owen,' said the High Commissioner kindly.

Yes, he should! He was Head of the Khedive's Secret Police, damn it!

All the same, a car! There were, now that the War had ended, a few in Cairo, but not many.

'I've never had a car before,' he confided.

'Well, now's your chance. You can have one of your own. And ride at the front of the procession.'

Golden visions swam before Owen's eyes.

But, then, at the very edge of the vision, a dark spot, rather like one of those spots that sometimes runs across in front of your eyes when you've got the lids closed.

'But, hey, if I'm at the front, they'll shoot me first!'

'There is that, of course,' agreed the High Commissioner.

◇◇◇

There was to be a procession the following Thursday and they had just been finalising the details. Owen had been against it from the first. For the past three weeks Cairo had been under a state of emergency and this, in Owen's view, was no time for processions. But the Khedive had been determined. Ever since the rejection of the two delegations (two, because Egypt had been unable to agree on a united approach) the Khedive had been looking for ways to put his nose back into joint. One of the delegations, led by the Prime Minister, had been his; the other, led by the leader of the Opposition, had not. In the end it had made no difference because Britain had declined to receive either delegation, whereupon Egypt had exploded.

There had been rioting in the streets and demonstrations in the university. Windows had been smashed and Europeans stoned. So far, not too bad. Owen was used to such things. But then people had been killed. Some Armenians had been picked on, as they often were, and some Copts attacked, as was not infrequently the case, too; but then some Civil Servants had been stabbed. They were English, and this was serious.

The Army had at once been brought in. The soldiers had been looking forward to being demobbed, now that the War had ended, and were not best pleased, so that the rioters had been handled roughly. That, of course, had brought more rioters on to the streets.

It was at this point that the Khedive, Egypt's ruler, had decided to display his authority. Hence the procession.

'It's lunacy,' said Owen, when he got back to his office.

Nikos, the Official Clerk, rather agreed with him; but then, Nikos was a Copt. The Copts, who had a talent for bureaucracy, had been running Egypt for about three thousand years under a succession of occupying powers, Pharaohs, Greeks, Arabs, Turks, French, and British, and they thought they knew something about the way things worked in Egypt. So did Willoughby, the

High Commissioner, but he hadn't been as long in his job. He was in favour of the procession.

'It will calm things down,' he said. 'We'll have troops everywhere, and it will remind people of the realities of the situation.'

Owen was rather afraid that it would.

◇◇◇

'Georgiades wants to see you,' said Nikos.

'Tell him to come in,' said Owen, going on into his office.

A fat, unhealthy-looking Greek appeared in the doorway.

Georgiades was one of Owen's agents and mostly he slouched around Cairo doing nothing. This was invaluable, since he picked up a lot of information that way.

'There's going to be a procession,' he said.

'Yes, I know.'

'The Khedive is going to drive round Cairo with his Ministers.'

'I know.'

Georgiades wandered across the room and perched himself on the edge of Owen's desk.

'The Khedive's not too popular at the moment.'

'No.'

'Nor are his Ministers.'

'True.'

'There's going to be an attempt to blow him up.'

'Is that definite?' said Owen, after a pause. 'Or just talk?'

Georgiades hesitated.

'Talk,' he said. 'But informed talk. I think we should take it seriously.'

'Go on,' said Owen.

'It's going to be in the Sharia Nubar Pasha. Just after the Midan Kanteret. Opposite the Hotel des Voyageurs.'

'That's very specific.'

'That's why we should take it seriously.'

'Who did you get it from?'

'Ali Baig.'

Owen nodded.

He knew Ali Baig. He could be relied upon.

He called Nikos.

'I heard,' said Nikos, getting up from his desk and coming through. 'What are you going to do?'

'Re-route. The procession will be going the usual way, up past the Ezbekiya Gardens. When it gets to the Midan Kanteret I'll lead it off down the Kanteret ed-Dekka.'

'*You'll* lead it off?'

'In my car,' said Owen, with an air of nonchalance.

◇◇◇

At the end of the morning he went to pick up Zeinab from the hospital where she worked. Work, in those leisurely days, finished for the day, at least in most Government offices, at two, when the whole city went into a slumber. It reawoke at four, when all the shops opened again, and then continued merrily until about three in the morning, which was, possibly, the reason why most Government officials, exhausted, went home early the next day.

Neither Owen nor Zeinab worked regular hours but, still in the first flush of their marriage, they liked to meet at midday twice a week and go home for lunch together and siesta afterwards. Owen was never able to sleep in the afternoon but now he had found something better to do than sleep and had developed a new enthusiasm for siesta.

There was an army car at the front of the hospital and in it was Zeinab. She waved to him but didn't get out and a moment later the car started up and weaved unsteadily round the square in front of the hospital. There was a soldier sitting in front alongside her and it was only after they had passed him that it occurred to Owen that it wasn't the soldier who was driving.

The car stopped and the solider got out and saluted.

'Your car, sir. I delivered it to your house but the lady said take it to the hospital so that she could try it.'

'*She* could try it?'

'Takes to it like a natural, sir.'

'I could drive you home,' said Zeinab optimistically.

Owen was new in experience of married life but old in experience of Zeinab and knew he would get nowhere by frontal objection.

'Where would we put it?' he said.

Since their marriage they had moved into an ancient Mameluke house in the old part of the city, a compromise between the poky bachelor flat that Owen was used to and the palatial quarters that Zeinab was used to (her father was a Pasha). The house was in a very narrow street. Its box-like meshrebiya windows on the upper floor almost touched those of the house opposite. There were no windows on the ground floor, which had security advantages. Since Owen was Chief of the Secret Police this mattered. There was, however, a door, a heavy wooden affair which led straight into a little courtyard.

Too little to put a car in, always supposing you could turn in the narrow, medieval street.

'Oh, you don't have to keep it, Sir,' said the driver. 'I'll look after it at the Barracks and pick you up whenever you require.'

'This is more like it,' said Zeinab happily, as they were driven home. 'It shows you're getting somewhere at last.'

Owen forbore to tell her exactly where it was getting him.

◇◇◇

Zeinab was putting the finishing touches to the dummy.

'That's my best suit,' Owen complained.

'This is a Royal procession, isn't it?'

'Yes, but suppose it gets messed up?'

'It won't be the only thing that gets messed up,' Zeinab pointed out, 'if the bomb goes off.'

'I don't like the sound of this,' said the driver.

'Oh, we'll be all right,' Owen assured him. 'It'll go off behind us—if it goes off at all.'

'All the same, sir, I think—if it's all right with you—I'll drop the car into the workshop when I get back and have a few extra armoured plates rigged up,' said the driver.

'Okay, but remember I, or, at least, the dummy, have got to be seen.'

The driver looked thoughtful.

'I know, sir,' he said, 'we'll have you sitting up high. While I'm sitting down low.'

Owen could see disadvantages in this.

'Don't forget, I've got to be able to get out quickly. Just before we put the dummy up.'

'Yes, sir, you get out. And I go on. Thank you very much, sir.'

'You'll be all right. You won't even be in the street when it's supposed to go off. But I will.'

Even Zeinab was struck now by doubts.

'Are you sure this is a good idea, darling?'

'No, it's a bloody bad idea. But it goes with the job.'

'Right, then,' said Zeinab, getting up. 'I'll be off to the hospital. I want to make sure we've got our emergency arrangements in place. For the casualties.'

◇◇◇

Owen was standing talking to Paul Trevelyan, the Oriental Secretary, in the forecourt of the Abdin Palace, watching the party assemble.

'It's lunacy,' Paul was saying. 'But, then, the whole thing's lunacy. They ought to at least have given them *something*. Not refused even to see them!'

'Couldn't you get them to see reason?'

'I tried. But everybody in London is focused on other things at the moment. There's a big Conference at Versailles about to come off and their minds are full of that. It's going to set the world right. At last. Or so the American President thinks, and he's a key mover. It will bring in democracy everywhere.'

'Oh, yes!' said Owen sceptically.

'More important, they'll all be staying in hotels in Paris. That's what their minds are really on. Paris! Whoopee! Egypt? Don't want to know about it.'

'It was like that, was it?'

'Exactly like that. And they wouldn't even let me go over to Paris myself to put our point of view! Bastards.'

Owen laughed.

'So what are we going to do now, Paul?'

'I've proposed they set up a Committee of Enquiry. They'll like that. It's the standard bureaucratic thing to do. It means they don't have to take a decision immediately.'

'But will Egypt accept it?'

'No. But they'll make such a to-do that it will probably persuade London that *they've* got to accept it.'

'And meanwhile?'

Paul looked around him at all the cars lining up.

'Meanwhile,' he said, 'we've got *this*.'

An elderly Egyptian in a smart European suit and a red fez came bustling across the forecourt towards them. He took Owen by both hands.

'My dear boy!' he said.

It was Zeinab's father.

'Hello, Nuri! Are you in on this jaunt, too?'

'No, no. I was asked but I thought…well, I thought better of it. I have just been explaining to Aban Taib that unfortunately other commitments—'

'And what did he say?'

'He said: 'Lucky sod!' And what about you, Mr. Trevelyan?'

'Unfortunately, I have other commitments too.'

'I haven't,' said Owen. 'Unlucky sod.'

'Ah, but you'll have the car,' said Nuri Pasha. 'Zeinab has been telling me about it. Why don't you bring it round, old boy? We could go for a spin.'

'Maybe, maybe.'

Nuri was glancing round.

'Ah, there's Rushdi Pasha. I think I'll have a word with him.'

Rushdi Pasha was the Prime Minister.

'I don't think it would be worth you having a word with him just now, Nuri Pasha,' said Paul.

Nuri was always trying to have a word with people in power. He still had lingering hopes of a recall to Ministerial office.

'He's tried to resign twice,' said Paul.

'Oh, yes, but the Khedive has turned him down. Insisted, positively insisted, that he stay.'

'I'll bet he wishes he were Zaghlul right now.'

Zaghlul Pasha was the Leader of the Opposition.

'Why, there is Zaghlul!' said Owen.

'Looking very unhappy,' said Paul. 'The Khedive has insisted that he be in the procession, too. It's not much of a safeguard but every little helps.'

Zaghlul saw them talking and came across.

'I hope you've got this all under control, Mamur Zapt,' he said to Owen.

'I'm just advisory, just advisory,' said Owen hurriedly.

That was the convenient fiction that sustained British power in Egypt: that the British officials there were just advisory. Beside every Egyptian Minister there was a British Advisor, beside every senior Egyptian official, a British one: just advising.

'No, you're not!' said Zaghlul Pasha. 'You're the exception. You're a direct appointee of the Khedive and responsible only to him.'

Well, not quite only. In practice. As Zaghlul knew very well. And the situation was unlikely to continue if, as seemed more than likely, Zaghlul came to power.

◇◇◇

The procession drove out through the Palace gates and into the vast Abdin Square, Owen's little car well out in front.

The Khedive was escorted as usual by a company of Egyptian cavalry, fine fellows all and immaculately turned out, very devils if it came to swords and lances but not quite so good against bombs and bullets. The cars had to drive slowly to allow the cavalry to keep up with them but at least, as Owen's driver remarked, they were a moving target.

Out in the middle of the huge square they were a long way from the crowds around its sides, but soon they turned into the Sharia Abd-el-Aziz, which, although one of the biggest streets in Cairo, was still a little too narrow for Owen's comfort. Both sides of the street were lined with soldiers, immaculate again, in their blue uniforms, fezzes, and white puttees. For the most part they were Sudanis, great, tall men and carrying unusually long ugly-looking bayonets which, Owen hoped, would put the fear of God into any unruly-minded spectators.

Not, apparently, too much need for that at the moment. Cairenes loved a spectacle and the crowds, kept well back behind the soldiers, were all cheering and applauding.

Apart from Owen and his driver there wasn't an Englishman in sight. The High Commissioner had prudently stopped at home. This, it was hoped to convey, was a purely Egyptian occasion, which maybe would reduce the risk of hostilities.

In fact, there were plenty of British soldiers around but they were kept discreetly off-stage, away from the streets the procession would pass through, but not so far away that they couldn't be deployed en masse and very quickly should the need arise.

They came to the Place Ataba-el-Khadra, usually thronging with people (since this was the main bus terminus of Cairo) and vehicles—carts and carriages—and animals—donkeys, camels, and tame sheep being fattened domestically for Passover, in bright ribbons and blue paint and running wild, always getting between people's legs. Today they had been cleared away, and round the square, alongside the soldiers, were the Cairo police, deployed when crowd control was necessary.

No problem here, either. Then off to the left past the Tribunaux Mixtes, the Opera, and the Ezbekiya Gardens; and then up right past the European hotels, first the Continentale and then Shepheard's, where trouble might have been expected. Garvin, the Commandant of the Cairo Police, had allowed for it and his big, truncheon-carrying policemen were everywhere. The terrace in front of Shepheard's was full of European sightseers, a tempting target on another occasion, particularly in the present emergency, but probably safe today with the terrorists having other plans.

They were coming up now to the Midan Kanteret, where Owen hoped to work his trick of an unexpected re-routing of the procession. It was a little square from which streets led off on all sides. That, too, was crowded with policemen, and

Garvin himself was there, making sure that everything was going according to plan.

There, too, was the Deputy Commandant, McPhee, and that was a bit of a worry. McPhee was an eccentric and one could never be certain that he wouldn't add an embellishment of his own to proceedings. He had been in Egypt for a long time and was blindly loyal to the Khedive. In fact, he was blindly loyal to most things, a Boy-Scoutish sort of man, which was all very well but in a place like Cairo, where ambiguities abounded and probably needed to be cultivated, not always a man you would want in a position of responsibility. On this occasion, fortunately Garvin would have him firmly in hand.

The Sharia Nubar Pasha, up which the procession had originally been intended to pass, turned off to the right. It, too, was lined with the troops but it was narrower than the streets they had been through and the soldiers were pressed back against the sides, which were all built up. A bomb could easily be thrown, although that, if Georgiades' information was correct, was not what was intended. Owen hoped that the terrorists hadn't changed their plans, too.

He moved out into the middle of the Midan and then stood up in the car and turned round and pointed as emphatically as he could down the Sharia Kanteret ed-Dekka, which was the direction he wanted. When he was sure the car behind had seen him, he sat down again and his car began to drive slowly along the Kanteret.

Glancing back, he saw that Garvin had intelligently swung a line of policemen across the entrance to the Nubar Pasha, blocking it off.

He saw also that the procession was beginning to follow him down the Kanteret.

'Okay,' he said to the driver, 'this is it!'

The car slowed right down. Owen opened the door and sprang out. He pushed through the line of soldiers and the people behind them and stepped into a shop front.

Looking back, he saw that the driver had immediately lifted the dummy into position and was driving on.

The procession was following him. He saw the Khedive's car go past.

Then he turned and went into the shop behind him.

'Police! Back door!' he snapped, and pushed on through.

Someone was quick-witted enough to open a door for him. He went through and found himself in a narrow, refuse-strewn alley way. He went up it and found another one going off to the right. He ran up that, his feet squelching in the rotten vegetation and the excrement, and found himself coming out on to the Sharia Nubar Pasha.

He forced his way through the puzzled people standing there and between the soldiers and then out on to the street.

For a moment, stepping out into the sunshine, he couldn't see anything but then, further up the street, he saw it. A water-cart, going ahead of the procession to sprinkle the street and keep the dust down, appeared to have broken down.

He saw Georgiades running towards it and began to run himself.

Two men jumped off the cart and began to run away.

'Get them! Get them!' he shouted.

They tried to break through the line of soldiers and policemen but were seized. One of the men twisted away and then ran off up a side alley. The other man ran into a huge policeman who picked him up and rammed his head against the underside of some box windows jutting out across the street. He rammed him again, and then again.

'Okay, Selim!' called Owen. 'That will do!'

Georgiades was bent over the water-cart. Owen went up to him. He had his hand down besides the driver's seat. As Owen approached, he brought his hand up and showed him something. It was a small glass bottle.

'It should be all right now,' he said. 'Just don't drop anything.'

'We're not moving it,' said Owen. 'We'll get someone else to do that who knows what they're doing.'

He looked along the street to where there was a police sergeant, standing stupefied. He beckoned him over.

'Get your boys to keep everyone back,' he said. 'There's a bomb in that cart. It should be all right now but we don't want to take any chances. Oh, and send one of your men back to the Midan Kanteret with this.'

He took out his notebook, scribbled a few words, tore the sheet out and gave it to the sergeant.

'Tell him to give it to Garvin Effendi.'

The sergeant, recovering, saluted and hurried off.

Next, Owen went over to the soldiers, who had been watching, wide-eyed.

'Is there a corporal here?'

'Sir!'

'There's a bomb in that cart. Get your men to help the police to keep everyone back.'

'What about the procession? There's a procession—'

'It's been diverted. It's not coming. Now you get on and help the police.'

'Got to stay where we are, sir, until we get orders.'

'You've *got* orders. Now bloody get on with it!'

The corporal was still standing there, apparently in a state of shock.

One of the other soldiers pulled at his arm.

'Come on, Mohammed, let's get on with it.'

'Yes, but—'

'He's the Mamur Zapt. That's good enough for the Khedive and that's good enough for the likes of you and me.'

The corporal still stood there, stunned. Several of the soldiers were already helping the police, however. The corporal allowed himself to be dragged in to join them.

Two men had followed the man who had run off up the alleyway. One of them now came hurrying back.

'Sorry, Effendi, he got away. I had just about got my hands on him when somebody blocked me. We followed him up to the end of the alley-way but then he disappeared. Talal's looking around for him now.'

'Pity. You go back and help him. At any rate we've got the other one. Selim!'

'Effendi!'

'Bring him over here.'

The big policeman had the other man firmly in a lock.

'All right,' said Owen, 'what's your name?'

'Hussein,' said the man sullenly.

'And the name of the other?'

Hussein kept his lips closed tightly.

'Were you driving the water-cart?'

'No.'

'So he was. And the people back at the depot will know his name. So you can tell me.'

'Ahmet.'

'Where will I find him?'

'I don't know.'

'The depot will know,' said Georgiades, materialising suddenly beside Owen.

'Get up there, will you? And take Zeid with you.'

'What about this one?' said Selim.

'Take him to the Bab-el-Khalk. I'll be along in a minute.'

He looked down the street. The police and the soldiers had the crowd under control, keeping them well back from the water-cart.

It was a standard city water-cart. Smart of them to use it. No one would question a water-cart going down the road ahead of the procession to spray the dust down.

McPhee came running up.

'Can I be of assistance, Owen?'

'You certainly can. Can you see that the people are kept well away from the cart?'

'Is that where it is?'

'It should be all right now. But we'd better make sure.'

'Garvin has sent back to the barracks for a bomb disposal team but it will be some time before they get here.'

'Can you look after things meanwhile? We've got one of the men and I want to question him.'

He took a last look along the street. A little old lady, English, had somehow got through the soldiers and gone up to the horses. She appeared to be feeding them lumps of sugar.

'Excuse me, Madam…'

She blinked up at him in a scared sort of fashion, as if she knew he was going to tell her off.

'They like them, you know. And it doesn't really do them any harm.'

'Madam, there's a bomb in that cart.'

'Bomb?' She looked at him uncomprehendingly.

'Yes. Just get back into the crowd, please.'

She retreated a few steps. But then came back determinedly.

'But what about the horses?'

'I'll look after the horses. Now if you will just—'

'They ought not to be left like that. Not if there's a bomb.'

'They won't be. Now, if you could just—'

'Where's their driver gone?'

Owen knew he shoudn't get involved in daft conversations like this but once you were in, it was hard to get out, especially if you didn't want to be unkind, and he didn't want to be, to this cracked old lady.

'He shouldn't have left them like that!' she said indignantly. 'Not with all the people! And a bomb!'

'Yes, well—'

'Where is he?' she demanded.

'We're trying to find him.'

McPhee, unexpectedly, came to his aid.

'Hello, Miss Skiff. What are you doing here?'

'Hello, Mr. McPhee. Can you imagine what has happened. These horses have been abandoned. I had been watching them— the cart broke down just opposite me. And they have such nice faces! And then the drivers ran away and just abandoned them! And there's a bomb—'

'Good heavens! Well, we'll have to do something about that, won't we?'

McPhee, Owen reflected, was a lot better at this sort of thing than he was.

'Should we take them along to the Animal Mission, do you think?'

'Well, no. We'd better not. They might be needed to draw the cart when we've mended it. But I'll tell you what: if you could go back to the Mission and find some nose-bags for them, and we could lay our hands on some hay, I think they'd be quite happy standing here for a little time.'

Yes, McPhee was definitely better at this sort of thing than he was.

Miss Skiff went off trustingly.

There was always one of them, thought Owen.

Chapter Two

Overhead there were kite hawks circling. They circled watchfully, not testing the thermal currents for fun, as he imagined some of the other birds doing, but rapaciously, on the look-out forever for food. One of them detached itself from its circle and darted down very near him. He ducked away instinctively. They went for things that glittered, too: glass, buckles, buttons. Once one had even snatched the sunglasses off his face. Ever since, Owen had mounted a subdued holy war of his own against them.

In the river men were filling black goat-skin water bags. This was the poor man's water supply. When the bags were full, the men heaved them out and put them across their shoulders, like a yoke. Then they went off through the city bearing water to the poorer houses. There were, of course, no taps in the houses. There were fountains outside most of the mosques to provide for the worshippers' ritual ablutions and wells in some of the little squares, and there were occasional public pumps. There was, too, a new Water Plant piping decent drinking water to the houses of the rich.

But the Nile was the main source of Cairo's water and it was where the water-carts went to stock up with the water with which they sprayed the streets. Dust was a great problem in Cairo and the carts were out from dawn to dusk.

Except for the period beginning at noon, when the drivers, like the rest of the population, took siesta. The carts had all returned and were drawn up in neat rows, their horses left in the shafts ready for the afternoon's runs but now taking a break like their masters but, alas, not like them, in the shade.

In the Depot nothing was moving: but then Zeid came round the lines of water-carts with a short, grey-haired man. His name, he said, was Babikr and he was the Depot Manager.

'This is a bad business, Effendi,' he said, 'and will bring shame upon the Depot.'

'Unjustly,' said Owen, 'for is not the Depot known for the excellence of its work?'

'It was,' said the Depot Manager gloomily. 'But now it will be known as the place which harbours people who try to blow up the Khedive!'

'There are always rotten oranges in the pile,' said Owen.

'But who would have thought…' began the Manager, and shook his head.

'Did they have a name for being troublesome?' asked Owen.

'No, Effendi. Not at all. If they had, they wouldn't have been here. The work is sought after. It may not seem much to you, Effendi, but to a poor man—! All my drivers know that if they fall short there are many eager to take their place.'

'Perhaps then they keep their troublesomeness for when they are away from the Depot?'

'It may be so, Effendi. I do not know.'

'These are strange times,' said Owen, 'and many feel there is change in the air. Some rush to embrace it. Were these two men like that?'

'I know what you mean, Effendi, but—'

'Did they go to meetings? Talk much about how the world might be bettered?'

'Effendi, my men are humble men. They keep their eyes on the ground. Most of them are from outside Cairo and before they came here they worked in the fields. They knew that if you lifted your eyes from the furrow, the Pasha's man would mark you, and that was when the blow would fall. They are not men to question the way of the world.'

'That is what I would have thought. But why, then…?'

'Money, Effendi. That is what my men say. Strangers came and spoke among the men. They asked first who watered the roads about the Midan Kanteret. And when they learned that it was Ahmet and Hussein, they took them aside.'

'Do you know what was said?'

'No, Effendi. And afterwards Ahmet and Hussein were pleased, and Ahmet said: 'That will pay the rent for a bit.' So the men knew they had been promised money.'

'One is not promised money for nothing. What was it that they had to do?'

'That I do not know, Effendi. And nor do my men. For Ahmet and Hussein would not say. However, Effendi-'

'Yes?'

'I cannot believe that they agreed to do that terrible thing. I know them, Effendi, and I cannot believe… They are not good men, Effendi, that I acknowledge, but they are not bad men either. They would not have done a thing like this if they had known. They must only have been told part of it.'

'I hear your words.'

'Effendi, I would not have had this happen for all the world. How can I go about now among my friends and raise my head? That it should be my men, drivers from my Depot…'

◇◇◇

The men were coming up from the river with their water-bags. Strictly speaking, they ought not to have been here, since this was the Depot's land, and the free-lance bag men were frowned upon. But the bank sloped gently into the river at this point and from time immemorial people had walked into the river to fill their bags.

They saw him watching the hawks, which seemed to have gathered now at a spot about a half mile away and one of them said:

'That's the hammam in Shafik Street, Effendi. They dumped a fresh load there this morning and the hawks are taking their pick.'

The hammams were the public baths, much used in Cairo. Their water was heated by burning rubbish, these days refuse collected by the municipal carts, and often the refuse was piled near them in great mounds which smelt abominably.

'Shafik Street? That's behind the Kasr el Aini, isn't it?'

'That's right, Effendi. I was there this morning.' He looked at Owen curiously. 'You've come about that cart, have you, Effendi?'

'That's right.'

He was amazed, as he always was, how quickly news travelled in Cairo.

'It's not back yet.'

'The police will still be looking at it. But it's not the cart that I'm interested in, it's the men who were driving it.'

'You won't find them here, Effendi. They'll be making themselves scarce for a bit.'

'They don't need to worry.' Word might get back through the same bush telegraph. 'They're just the little people, the ones who get caught.'

'While the big ones get away with it. That's always the way with it, isn't it, Kemal?' he said to the man standing beside him. 'That's the way of the world.'

'Dead right,' said Kemal.

'It's the big ones I'm after,' said Owen. 'There was a bomb in that cart, a big one. It wouldn't only have been the Khedive that was killed.'

They didn't say anything but he hoped that the point had been registered.

He walked on a little way beside them.

Then—

'We saw them,' said the bag-man unexpectedly.

'Saw—?'

'The men who came here and talked to the drivers. We wondered what they were doing here. I thought maybe they were Babikr's bosses. But Kemal said they weren't. Too rich, he said.'

'Too rich?'

'It wasn't just their suits. They came in a car.'

'Not an arabeah?'

Arabeahs were the little, horse-drawn, fly-blown carriages which served as taxi-cabs in Cairo.

'No, not an arabeah. They left it waiting for them, Effendi, while they went about their business. Afterwards, we saw them get in.'

'A car of their own?'

'That's right, Effendi.'

The man looked at him significantly. Private carriages were much more common than private cars on the streets of Cairo.

'It must be a Pasha at least, I said to Kemal.'

'Dead right,' said Kemal.

'A car!' said Owen.

The man looked at him slyly.

'Not like you, Effendi!'

'No, not like me,' said Owen. 'Better than a lift on a water-cart, isn't it?'

The men laughed. Then they shifted the water-bags on their shoulders and went off.

◇◇◇

He saw Georgiades coming in through the depot gates, holding a man. The Greek was deceptive. He seemed fat and flabby but when he got his hands on you, they were surprisingly strong. He had an arm-lock on the man and there was little the man could do about it.

'Ahmet, is it?'

'What if it is?' the driver said, truculently.

Owen was pleased but surprised.

'I didn't really expect you to pick him up so easily,' he said to Georgiades.

'And you wouldn't have,' said the driver. 'Only I went back home to get some money. I didn't think you'd get there so quickly.'

'Well, there you are!' said Georgiades. 'I'm like that!'

He looked at Owen.

'What do you want me to do with him? Do you want to talk to him? Or shall I take him back to the Bab-el-Khalk?'

'No, not yet. Take him down to the river.'

He wanted to get him on his own, away from the other people.

'The river?'

Georgiades looked surprised, the driver apprehensive.

'Hey!' he said. 'What are you going to do to me?'

'There was a bomb in that cart.'

'Look, that was nothing to do with me.'

'You were driving the cart, weren't you?'

'Yes, but—'

'Didn't they tell you?'

'No, they bloody didn't! And if they had, I wouldn't have done it!'

'But you did do it, Ahmet, and that was bad. Ordinary people might have been killed. Women and children!'

'I don't know anything about that.'

'Got children of your own?'

'Yes, I have, as a matter of fact. And I'm telling you I wouldn't have done it—'

'—if you'd known. What did you know, Ahmet?'

The man closed his lips firmly.

'Nothing!' he said.

'How much did they offer you?'

Almet shook his head obstinately.

'Enough to pay the rent? That's what you said. And a bit more? Look, you can tell me that, Ahmet. I've talked to Hussein.'

'A bit more,' he muttered.

'What was it for, Ahmet? Was it to carry the bomb and let if off?'

'No, it bloody wasn't!'

'Tell me.'

'It was—'

Ahmet stopped.

'Just to carry the bomb?'

'No! No! I didn't know anything about the bomb!'

'Don't tell me they promised you all that money for doing nothing, Ahmet!'

'I'm not saying anything!'

'Why not, Ahmet? Because they told you not to? Threatened you, perhaps? Kept some of the money back? But, look, Ahmet, the way it is left means that you get all the blame. You're the one who will be punished. The bomb was in your cart. A bomb! The Khedive! Think, Ahmet, think! The punishment will be heavy. While they, the ones who spoke to you, suffer nothing. Is that fair, Ahmet?'

'Look, I know nothing about it.'

'Oh, come, Ahmet! They gave you money. What for? If it wasn't to carry the bomb?'

'It was…it was to break down. In the road the Khedive was to travel on. It was a sort of joke, see? That's what they told me. There were all those nobs, the Khedive and all that, all going along in their fancy cars, and they'd have to stop. It would make them look silly, see? Remind them who did the work around here. Show them how important a water-cart driver was. That was all! All I had to do was break down in the Sharia Nubar Pasha, where it would be awkward for them. That's what they said. That's what they told me. They didn't say anything about a bomb! God knows, if they had, I wouldn't have—'

'All right, all right. But, Ahmet, what about these men? These men who hold back, keep out of sight, and let you take the blame—what sort of men are they?'

'Posh. And not just ordinary posh, if you know what I mean. Not like Ali Bakhtar, say, who runs the big shop in the bazaar. *Really* posh. The way they were dressed! Like the Khedive himself! As if they were wrapped in money. Their shoes—'

Ahmet shook his head in wonderment.

'Their shoes?'

'Shone like the sun! And you could see they didn't have to polish them or anything. And their hair!'

'What about their hair?'

'It smelt of roses.'

'I see.' He thought for a moment. 'And did they wear the tarboosh?'

The pot-like red hat that almost all officials wore. Owen himself wore one.

'Oh, yes, Effendi.'

That was foolish of them, thought Owen. But then, there were a lot of officials in Cairo.

◇◇◇

He told Georgiades to take Ahmet back to the Bab-el-Khalk. He was not, however, going with him. He had one more visit he wanted to pay first: to the Mission for Sick Animals. Actually, they didn't have to be sick. Any animal would do, but it helped if it was in need of care and protection.

As, of course, most animals in Cairo were. Donkeys were often overloaded and always being beaten. Camels, difficult beasts and particularly difficult in towns, were always stopping in the narrow streets and blocking up passage for everyone until they were whipped into continuing. Oxen proceeded under a general hail of blows, and even the docile horses that pulled the arabeahs were treated with casual brutality. It wasn't so much, as some maintained, that Orientals were cruel, as that life generally was cheap.

There was no denying, though, that animals in Cairo were ill-treated and this had roused the concern of the redoubtable ladies who had formed the Mission. They patrolled the streets in search of animals which needed their assistance and then seized them from their astonished owners, sometimes paying for them, which astonished the owners even more, and took them to the Mission for rehabilitation. It was a cause that Owen could commend, but hitherto he had not felt moved to engage with the Mission more closely.

Its office was in a small back-street not far from the Midan Kanteret and at first he was surprised to see so few animals there. That was because, a sturdy, grey-haired lady informed him, they were at once transferred to more sympathetic surroundings outside the city where they could benefit from green fields and medical attention. The base in the City was just a forward point from which the Mission's patrols could push out in all directions.

And were the patrols out even now? They were indeed. And Miss Skiff with them? Miss Skiff had not long returned and was sitting outside in the small courtyard having a cup of tea.

'Miss Skiff! Captain Owen. I have come to see that you have got back safely.'

'Thank you. That is most kind of you. As you see, I have. Mr. McPhee was kind enough to bring me.'

'And were you able to procure some nose-bags for the horses?'

'I was. We always have some lying around. It helps to calm the horses after someone has brought them.'

'Ah, good. And the hay—?'

'I have a young friend who helped to find some. Ah, here he is!'

A young Egyptian boy came into the courtyard.

'This is Hillal.'

'Greetings to you, Hillal.'

'And to you, Effendi, salaams.'

'Hillal is a former pupil of mine. A very good pupil, I may add.'

Hillal smiled.

'All Miss Skiff's pupils were good pupils,' he said affectionately.

'But not as good as Hillal,' said Miss Skiff fondly. 'He was always so helpful. I felt he had a natural talent for the classroom. I tried to persuade him to become a pupil teacher, but it was not to be.'

'I have brothers and sisters, Effendi,' Hillal explained, 'and my mother is alone. She needs the money.'

'And a pupil teacher is paid so little,' said Miss Skiff.

'Perhaps I can help?' suggested Owen. 'There are grants for this kind of thing and perhaps if my voice were added to Miss Skiff's…'

Hillal shook his head regretfully.

'It would not be enough, Effendi. And it would take all my time whereas at the moment I can do many things, small things, which add up.'

'He works so hard,' said Miss Skiff. 'And yet he still helps me with the Mission.'

'The Prophet tells us that each day we should try to do some good,' said the boy seriously. 'Well, this is my good. And, besides,' he shrugged. 'I like horses.'

'Are the horses back at the Depot yet?' asked Miss Skiff.

'No. Not yet. I have just been down there. To check on the conditions there.'

'Oh, they're not bad at the depot,' Miss Skiff said brightly. 'I've been down there myself. No, it's when they get out on the streets—the drivers are sometimes so unmerciful. But there's no point in beating them, is there? It's not as if they're in a race.'

'Indeed not. And I hope that the drivers of the cart in the Nubar Pasha were not ill-treating their horses?'

'No, they weren't ill-treating them. They were not exactly kind to them but I've seen a lot worse.'

'It wasn't their fault that the cart broke down.'

'No. And, to do the men justice, I don't think they pretended it was, which drivers do sometimes, you know. One of the men got down and looked under the cart, and then he said something to the other man, and then the other man jumped down and they both ran away.'

'Ah, he looked under the cart, did he?'

'Yes, as if something was broken. But it seemed all right to me. It was going along quite normally and then it stopped. For no reason that I could see. And then the men ran away, leaving the horses standing there. Of course, they're used to it, so normally it wouldn't matter. But with so many people around, and the street so narrow, it didn't seem to me right. I spoke to the man beside me and said: 'They shouldn't leave them like that!' 'No, they shouldn't,' he said. 'Not with the Khedive coming. They should get that bloody cart out of the way.' 'Which was not what I meant.'

'You did see the drivers, of course?'

'Of course.'

'Would you recognise them if you saw them again?'

'I think so.'

'It's just that you may be asked to identify them. If it's decided to take action against them.'

'Well, I wouldn't want to see them actually punished. Although I do think they shouldn't be allowed to drive around carrying a bomb. Not with so many people around. And the horses so near.'

◇◇◇

As he walked back to the Bab-el-Khalk he felt reasonably satisfied. The Khedive was safe and should be back in the Abdin Palace by now. He had two of the men responsible and they had told him interesting things which would, he thought, allow him to get the others. He would get more out of them when he got back to the Bab-el-Khalk. The shock of being in the cells often loosened tongues. All in all it had been a pretty good day.

◇◇◇

He had hardly got into his office when Nikos said:

'There's a man to see you.'

'Can he wait? I want to talk to that man we arrested first.'

'This is his lawyer.'

'His *what?*'

Drivers of municipal water-carts didn't have lawyers. Not in Cairo, they didn't.

'A Mr. Narwat. He says he has been retained by Hussein Farbi.'

'Look, he can't have been. We've only just taken Farbi in.'

'Nevertheless.'

'He hasn't had time to retain him. Has he sent a message out?'

'No.'

'Then this is a fix. Tell him to sod off.'

'Mr. Narwat is a respectable, well-known lawyer,' Nikos said neutrally.

'He *can't* have been retained.'

'He says he has been. I think,' said Nikos, 'that you'd better see him.'

◇◇◇

Mr. Narwat, a short, balding Egyptian in a dark suit, bustled in and held out his hand.

'Captain Owen? I'm Yasin Narwat and I'm representing Hussein Farbi, whom I believe you are holding?'

'That's right, yes.'

'Have you charged him yet?'

'Not had a chance to.'

'Ah, well, we're only dealing with formalities, then. I need not take up much of your time.'

'I was hoping to ask him a few questions.'

Mr. Narwat pursed his lips.

'Well, you certainly can. But I shall advise him to confine his answers to giving his name and address.'

'This was nearly a serious incident. Innocent lives could have been lost. Including those of women and children.'

Mr. Narwat pursed his lips again.

'Appalling!' he said.

'I was hoping that Mr. Farbi would be able to help me in my inquiries.'

'I am sure he would wish to do so. However…'

'You don't think he will be able to?"

'I am afraid I would have to advise him otherwise. In his own interests. May I be present while you charge him?'

Owen shrugged.

'Tell Selim to bring him up,' he said to Nikos.

'And Mr. Ahmet Kassani, too,' said Mr. Narwat quietly.

'Separately,' said Owen.

◇◇◇

Selim appeared with Hussein.

'Ah, Mr. Farbi? I am Yasin Narwat and I shall be representing you.'

'What?' said Hussein.

'I am your lawyer,' said Mr. Narwat patiently.

'My—?'

'But what is this?' Mr. Narwat cut him off. 'My client appears to be suffering from injury!'

'Received while resisting arrest.'

'So the police always say!'

'There were witnesses at the time.'

'But not to what went on afterwards in the cells.'

'Nothing went on afterwards in the cells.'

'No? Well, well, Captain Owen, perhaps we don't need to make too much of this. I shall, of course, be applying for bail.'

'Bail?' said Owen incredulously. 'On a charge like this?'

'It is, of course, up to you whether you oppose it. But in view of the possible question of violence inflicted while in police custody…'

He paused, leaving the threat, or offer, dangling in the air.

Owen could read his game now.

He smiled.

'I'll think about it,' he said.

◇◇◇

'Violence?' protested Selim, after Narwat had gone and Hussein had been returned to the cells. 'He just jumped up in my hands and hit his head on the underneath of the meshrebiya above! That's all it was!'

But how would that sound in court, Owen wondered?

The speed with which the lawyers had been deployed troubled him. He was beginning to realise that there was more to this than he had thought.

◇◇◇

The bomb consisted of a piece of iron piping with screw-cap ends enclosing a metal container filled with picric acid. Inside the lips of one end of the piping was hung a small glass bottle containing nitric acid, closed with a loose plug of cotton-wool. So long as the bomb was kept upright it was harmless but once out of the vertical the nitric acid oozed into the picric and detonated it.

'Not the usual sort of thing, sir,' said the sergeant at the barracks. 'The man who dreamed this up wasn't exactly what I would call a professional, sir. I've got a dozen better bits of kit in my store. If you wanted to blow someone up, that is. This was an amateur job. But not an ignorant amateur. It was someone who knew something about science. Not a lot, perhaps, but enough.'

Owen nodded.

'I've seen something like this before,' he said.

The sergeant looked at him shrewdly.

'A student, sir? They're up to all kinds of tricks, aren't they? And this would be within the capacity of even a first year student in one of the Science Departments. And just at the moment, the way things are in Cairo…'

◇◇◇

While he was at the Barracks he went round to see his car. He found the driver polishing it.

'It's got a bit dusty, sir,' he said apologetically.

He gestured at the extra armoured plates he had had put in.

'Want these taken out, sir? I imagine there'll be no need for them now.'

How wrong!

◇◇◇

'I don't know what you're fussing about,' said Zeinab. 'You can always get it cleaned.'

While he was at the garage he had picked up his suit. Its state was less than pristine.

'It looks all right to me,' said Zeinab.

'Yes, but it's as if someone else has worn it.'

'Heavens, it was only a dummy!'

But Owen still felt uncomfortable.

'It's my best suit,' he said lamely.

'It's your *only* decent suit. And it's high time you get another one.'

'What with?'

'It's nearly the end of the month, isn't it?'

For Zeinab the glass was always half full.

'There are still ten days to go. And there are all those things you bought last week that we haven't paid for yet.'

'They'll give you credit. Someone in your position.'

Zeinab brought assumptions to their marriage which she had carried over from life with her father. Nuri Pasha had always lived in style. That, as he said, was half the battle. The other half, of course, was finding the wherewithal to pay for it, and this had always proved more difficult. Business, he knew he had no great capacity for. For Government, on the other hand, he was sure he had: at least, for that capacity to turn office into favours into cash that had always marked out the Ministers of the old Regime.

And, indeed, when he had had his chance, he had not done too badly, in that respect at least. Unfortunately, over one crucial issue, which became known as the Denshewai Incident, and which had ever after loomed large in Nationalist political mythology, he had backed the wrong side: the British. He had lost power and never regained it. But he had always lived in hopes it would return; and never more than at the present moment when the political situation was so fluid and so many things had suddenly become uncertain.

Unfortunately, he had lived in hopes for quite some time now and the hopes had always hitherto been disappointed. Including the hope of being able to rectify his financial position.

Zeinab had inherited something of her father's disposition and acquired something of his approach to life. It was not that she cared particularly about money; it was just that she took its existence for granted. Even when there was none. She had grown up all her life in the illusion of being rich.

Her mother had never shared that illusion. She had been Nuri's favourite courtesan and he had loved her beyond reason. He had even, to the shock of all Cairo, offered to marry her. He had been even more shocked when she had refused him. Strong-willed and independent-minded, she had insisted on their maintaining separate households, probably wisely so far as financial matters went.

When she died she left Zeinab a very considerable sum but as it took the traditional form of gold in a box under the bed, and Zeinab, who revered her mother, had adamantly refused to make any change in this, the Owens still had difficulty in paying the rent. Owen, like all Civil Servants in Egypt, was paid a pittance, and, as he refused to augment his income in the way usual among Government officials, they barely scraped along.

When the War hadn't looked like resolving itself without her efforts, Zeinab had determined to do her bit. She had decided to become a nurse. This had offended both Egyptian men and British ladies, the men because they didn't believe in women working anywhere outside the house and the brothel, the British ladies because they didn't believe in having Egyptian women working alongside them. Zeinab had been turned down. Roused, she had shown a capacity for in-fighting which had impressed even her father's political cronies.

It had also impressed Cairns-Grant, the doyen of the medical world in Cairo and the man who actually ran the hospital, never mind what his formal position was. In the difficult circumstances of war-time Egypt, with the flood of military casualties come in from Gallipoli, he had needed a strong, ruthless administrator to take some of the load off his shoulders and thought that he had found one. He had appointed Zeinab as his Senior Administrative Assistant and ridden rough-shod over every objection.

And he had not been disappointed. Zeinab had taken to the work in a manner that had astonished her father, delighted the radical female Islamic world of Cairo (there was one), and enraptured the patients, most of whom were Australians, hitherto unimpressed by military management. The appointment had been a great success.

But it had not resulted in a great improvement in Zeinab's financial position. Partly this was because the salary was low, partly that Zeinab, who had never bothered to find out exactly what it was, did not appreciate how low it was. She had continued with her cavalier treatment of the relation between income and expenditure.

But then, as she pointed out, this was no different from the country's practice in general.

The question was, as Owen pointed out in return, frequently, how long this could continue. And there was a new edge to the question given the different situation created by the end of the War and the new hopes of Egypt. As the flow of military patients dried up, would the hospital be closed down? Even if it wasn't, could it continue to be administered in the present way? Was it right that so much should be governed by the decree of the senior doctor? Was it acceptable to Muslim opinion that there should be a woman—Yes! a woman!—assisting him in such a prominent position?

And behind this there were lots of other questions. Would there be a new Government which would take a completely different line from previous ones? What would be its attitude to the British occupation—sorry, British assistance? To the presence in the country of so many British officials? To a British Mamur Zapt overseeing the country's internal security? To the continuance of the Khedive himself?

Egypt, everyone sensed, was changing and that would affect everything and everybody.

Chapter Three

The next morning someone came from the Khedive.

'His Royal Highness demands an explanation for the diversion of the Procession yesterday morning.'

'We learned that there was to be an attempt on his Highness' life.'

'An attempt on—but this is serious!'

'Yes.'

'Why was His Highness not informed?'

'His Highness had been previously informed that going ahead with the Procession could lead to dangerous incidents and had been advised to cancel or postpone it. However, His Highness had chosen to overrule the advice.'

'Yes, but that warning was general. Had you learned of a specific threat?'

'Yes.'

'Then why was not His Highness informed of that? And why did you not do something about that, instead of disrupting the whole Procession?'

'We knew only that the attempt was to be made in the Sharia Nubar Pasha, but we didn't know exactly where. I thought it best to take no chances and divert the Procession along the Kanteret-ed-Dekka.'

'In doing so you deprived his loyal subjects at the Gare Centrale and the Gare Pont-Limousin of the opportunity to express their love for their Khedive and His Highness is gravely displeased.'

'I am sorry.'

'Consider yourself reprimanded.'

Owen bowed his head.

The official half turned to go but then wavered.

'What—what exactly was the nature of the threat?' he asked.

'A bomb. Big enough to kill the Khedive.'

'How frightful!'

'And anyone nearby. Bombs don't discriminate. There would have been women and children in the crowd.'

'Shocking!'

'Of course, it was probably aimed more at the officials and Ministers following in the cars immediately behind.'

'But I was in one of those cars!'

'It could have been intended, I think, as a blow against the whole Government. A sort of Gunpowder Plot.'

'Gunpowder—?'

'A plot to blow up the entire English Parliament with barrels of gunpowder stored in the cellars.'

'Good heavens! And you think that yesterday—?'

'Sort of. Yes.'

'Gunpowder Plot?'

'A figure of speech, but—'

The official pulled himself together.

'I don't think this is an occasion for figures of speech, Mamur Zapt. If they're like that. Consider yourself doubly reprimanded.'

◇◇◇

Zeid came back to report. He had done well. Motor cars were not so common a sight in the part of town where the Water Depot was located as to pass unnoticed and much of the local population had come out to inspect the car. The driver—there had been a driver, which was significant in itself—torn as he was between the desire to show off his charge and an urgent need to defend it against the preying hands of the local children, had fought a hard battle.

It was one of the latter, however, who had furnished Zeid with the most useful description of the vehicle: it was, the boy said, a modified De Dion.

Encouraged by Zeid, he had volunteered that it was a very special car and that he had only seen one previously; and that was practicing on the track at Helwan. There was to be a race at the weekend and in his opinion it was a toss-up between the De Dion and the Brazier.

The intelligent Zeid had decided to go out to Helwan and pursue his inquiries there but first, he had thought, he had better report in at the Bab-el-Khalk. On his way an idea had struck him. This was a very distinctive car: might it not be known at the Automobile Club?

The Automobile Club had been established only the year before. It was a very exclusive establishment, since only the rich had private cars. Rich and, in Zeid's opinion, foolish; foolish enough to risk crashing their acquisition in the race meetings which had sprung up at Helwan. But that appeared to be the sort of person who might own a De Dion.

The Club was, alas, too exclusive to answer the inquiries of one such as Zeid. However, he had gone round the back and talked to some of the servants and found out that there was, indeed, a De Dion owner among the Club's members. His informant was not sure of the owner's name. But he was a Prince at least and lived at the Palace.

Zeid knew, of course, that in the mind of the average Cairene anyone rich lived at the Palace. He had thought, however, that there was sufficient possibility of this being true for him to go to the Palace and see what he could find out there.

The Palace was less exclusive a place than the Automobile Club and he had found it easy to gain entrance and talk to people. But what he soon discovered was that within the Palace there were inner walls through which it was difficult to penetrate. The walls were invisible but manned by people fiercely loyal to the Khedive, who, after Zeid had pressed his inquiries for a while, took to ostentatiously fondling the daggers at their belts, whereupon Zeid judged that it was time to go.

As he left, however, he took the opportunity to visit the Royal garages, where, of course, he found any number of motor-cars. Among them was one which he thought might be a De Dion: but when he inquired about this, the garage mechanics closed up like clams and, soon after, one of the bedaggered men he had previously encountered hurried towards him.

◇◇◇

Owen was sitting in his office thinking about this when the telephone rang. It was Paul Trevelyan.

'Gareth, what's this? Why haven't we been told?'

'Told what?'

'About this attempt to blow up the Palace.'

'Palace?'

'A veritable Gunpowder Plot, so we've been told.'

'Just a minute, just a minute!'

'The Khedive's been on to us this morning. Blaming us. And you, of course, but that doesn't matter.'

'Look—'

'Worse, he's been on to London, too. And *they've* been on to us. The Old Man's running round in circles.'

'Look, if this is what I think it is, it's a storm in a tea-cup.'

'An attempt to blow up the Abdin Palace? And the Khedive with it? Jesus, Gareth, I admire sang-froid, but isn't this carrying it to extremes? Look, for you this may be the equivalent of a quiet day on the North-West Frontier, or wherever the hell you were before you came to Egypt, but for us in dull old Cairo it's not something you just casually brush aside—'

'Hold on, hold on! I think there's been some confusion here. So far as I know, there's been no attempt to blow up the Palace.'

'No attempt to blow up the Palace?'

'No.'

'What the hell are they talking about, then?'

'The bomb, I think.'

'Oh, just a bomb? That's all right, then.'

'The Procession yesterday. There was a bomb. But we sorted it out. Actually, I think I can see how the confusion may have arisen. I made a casual reference to the Gunpowder Plot—'

'Just the thing to mention to a jumpy Khedive at the moment!'

'—and it got blown up—'

'Gareth!'

'—Exaggerated,' Owen hastily corrected himself. 'Exaggerated. Out of all proportion. What I said was twisted.'

There was a silence at the other end of the phone.

'You mean there's been no attempt to blow up the Palace?'

'Not as far as I know.'

'No Gunpowder Plot?'

'Well, plot, perhaps. In fact, I wanted to speak to you about that. But not taking quite this form.'

'Gareth, there you go again. You're taking things much too calmly. What's a little plot among friends? Unless, of course, it's aimed at you. The Khedive's going crazy, the High Commissioner's going crazy, London's going crazy—'

'I thought you wanted to bring Egypt to London's attention?'

'Yes, but—Christ!'

Another silence. Then, 'I suppose there is something in that,' said Paul grudgingly.

'In what?'

'It could bring it to their attention.'

Then, more positively, 'Yes, there definitely is something in that. Or could be. Do you know, I think it might be possible to get something out of this. A Royal Commission, at least.'

He began to sound distinctly cheerful.

'Yes, I really think so. I'll get on to them right away. If there's one thing any Government takes seriously, it's an attempt to blow a Government up. You know, I really think this could work to our advantage. In the end.'

'Paul.'

'Yes, I really think so.'

'Paul.'

'Yes?'

'I think I've got a bit of a problem.'

'But I thought you said—?'

'No, it's okay. Everything's contained. But it's where I think my investigation may be leading to.'

'Where might it be leading to?'

'The Palace. I think.'

'You mean—?'

'That's where the plot started. I think.'

There was a silence.

'Sure?'

'Not yet.'

'Come back when you've got something more to go on. I don't want to involve the Old Man too early. Especially with the Commission in the offing.'

'Okay, I'll come back.'

Paul paused.

'The Palace, you say?'

'Yes.'

'Hum.' Then, cheerfully: 'Well, there are always plots in the Palace. You'll sort things out, I'm sure.'

'And I've been reprimanded. Formally. The Khedive sent someone round.'

'Oh, well,' said Paul carelessly, 'what's one reprimand among so many? Or it would have been many if they had found out.'

◇◇◇

Owen sat at a table outside a restaurant in the Ataba al Khadra watching the world go by. There was plenty of it. The Ataba was the main terminus for most of the new electric trams of Cairo, as well as for most of the buses. The buses were large, slow, open carts usually crammed with black-gowned women carrying baskets. They all got off together and then stood talking in the middle of the road, which was possibly unwise, since while the trams usually stopped here, they certainly wouldn't stop for them.

Add to that the fact that some of the main streets of Cairo debouched into the square, bringing with them carts full of heavy stores for the dam, forage camels piled high with mountains of green fodder, porters carrying as much as a camel, arabeahs and the occasional motor car, and you got some idea of the hazards.

Not that any of these objects could move very fast, for the square was full of people: passers through like the black-gowned ladies, or people not passing at all but just standing and chatting, street vendors selling everything from peanuts to dirty postcards and virulent nationalist newspapers, and particularly sticky sweets and pastries, carried precariously on large trays and coated with what seem a black layer of film but was actually flies. And shoeblacks and sheep. The shoeblacks were mostly little boys who were everywhere. Stand still a moment and you found your feet being brushed. The sheep were mostly fat-tailed sheep, with tails like bladders full of melted lard, silver necklaces around their necks (they were treated as pets until the Passover feast) and painted affectionately in all the colours of the rainbow.

Into this melée suddenly came marching a long procession of students. They were chanting Nationalist songs and slogans and were on their way to the High Commissioner's, outside whose establishment they were going to parade and shout their defiance.

There would be police there, and soldiers, and as long as they kept to chanting and slogans, there would be no bother. But it was always touch and go these days. It could so easily tip into violence. Opinion in the expatriate community was divided over what you should do about this. Many were in favour of putting them down. 'Jump on them, jump on them, Owen!' He knew they were saying it at the Sporting Club. But he didn't want to jump on them. Cracking down, in his experience, always led to more trouble. What you had to do was contain them somewhere and go on containing them until they got bored and went away. But he knew that view was unpopular.

The procession passed through the Ataba without incident. Not exactly smoothly because the crowds refused to make way and the students had to filter through before regrouping in the streets the other side. But it sorted itself out without violence, and that was really Owen's point.

The strategy was fine so long as it worked.

He was waiting for an old friend of his, Mahmoud el Zaki, a young Egyptian lawyer. They had started out in the Khedive's service at roughly the same time, Mahmoud in the Department of Prosecutions of the Ministry of Justice. The Egyptian legal system was modeled on that of the French and the Parquet, as the Department of Prosecutions was called, handled not just the prosecution in court but also the investigation. His job—setting aside the political and security aspects—was not unlike Owen's and the two had worked together on a number of cases.

Mahmoud was as sharp as a knife and had for some time been the Parquet's rising star. Lately, though, his upward trajectory had slowed down; indeed, it seemed to have hit the buffers. Mahmoud, like most young Egyptian professionals, was a member of the Opposition Wafd Party, the one led by Zaghlul, and Paul Trevelyan said that he was too much of a reformer for the old guard who had the say in the Ministry of Justice, as they did in the other Ministries. Mahmoud had been shunted off into some administrative by-pass and Owen wondered how long he would be content to stay like that.

He came now weaving through the tables, a smile on his face. They embraced affectionately in the Arab way. Then Mahmoud sat down and looked around for the waiter, which was *not* the Arab way. The last thing an Arab would do in a café was order coffee. He would wait for it to come, like manna from heaven, and meanwhile he would read the papers, play dominoes, or chat. The only thing he would do for the good of the house was, occasionally, to hire a pipe, since his own pipe, with its water jar and length of hose, was too large to carry around. Mahmoud, however, was a strict Muslim and did not smoke; he was at the same time a compulsive Westerner, in that he believed in getting on with things. The waiters here knew him and they knew Owen and pretty soon came over with small cups and a brass pot with a long spout and poured them both coffee.

They talked a little, in guarded terms, about the political situation, and then Owen got to the point. He told Mahmoud about the Royal Procession and the bomb, and then about Mr. Narwat.

'It is only right,' said Mahmoud mildly, 'that a defendant should be legally represented. Even a water-cart driver.'

'I have no objection to that. But would a water-cart driver normally be able to hire someone like Mr. Narwat?'

'Of course not. I know Yasin Narwat and he is very expensive. He may, mind you, be doing it for nothing. Lawyers sometimes do that in political cases. However—' he shook his head, '—I don't think Yasin Narwat is like that.'

'Someone else is paying. And I was wondering if word had got round who.'

Mahmoud shook his head again.

'I don't think so. Not yet, at any rate. I will keep my ears open.'

He sat for a moment, thinking.

'It is, however, a little surprising. That Narwat should let himself get involved in a thing like this. Even if he was *very* well paid. It's not the sort of thing that he usually touches. And that's nothing to do with politics, it's a social matter. He likes to stick with the well-to-do.'

'Well, he could still be doing that.'

Mahmoud looked at him quickly.

'He could?'

'This could—just could—be going right back to the Palace.'

'Well, that *is* interesting.' He took it in. 'So this could be big, then?'

'It could.' Owen waited and then said: 'You wouldn't like to come in on it, would you? I could ask for you to be assigned.'

Mahmoud shook his head regretfully.

'They wouldn't do it,' he said. 'They're keeping me tied up at a desk. In any case—'

He stopped.

'Yes?'

'I don't know.' He shook his head again. 'I don't know,' he said. Then he looked at Owen. 'The fact is, things could be about to change. If the Government falls and Zaghlul gets in. I've been told—just a hint, you understand? nothing firm—that if a new Administration is formed, I might be included.'

'Gosh!'

Owen rested back. This was something new. He hadn't realised that Mahmoud had reached these heights.

'Congratulations!' he said. 'If it comes.'

'It probably won't. It almost certainly won't. There are plenty of people who don't want it to happen. That may be,' he said ruefully, 'why I'm being blocked.'

'Look, I realise I shouldn't have spoken. Not in the circumstances. Sorry.'

'No, no. You weren't to know. And please keep it quiet. Don't even drop a hint.'

'No, no, of course not.'

'It may never happen.'

'They couldn't do better.'

'That's probably why it will never happen,' said Mahmoud, laughing.

◇◇◇

When Owen got home, Zeinab was full of something that had happened to her that morning. She had been sitting in her office at the hospital when a woman had come in: young, well dressed, in European style, although with a veil over her face which she had removed as soon as she had got in.

'I want a job,' she had said.

'Job?'

Zeinab was taken aback. Women didn't do this sort of thing in Egypt.

'Yes. In the hospital.'

'Are you a doctor?'

'No.'

'A nurse, perhaps?'

'No.'

'Well…'

And in any case, the nursing was done by men. It was true there had been women nurses during the War but they had been British. The ladies of the expatriate community had volunteered their services, eager to do their bit and Cairns-Grant, a little reluctantly but hard-pressed, had accepted them. But when the War ended they had quietly drifted away and been replaced by men.

'I want to work in an office. Like you, Zeinab.'

'Yes, well, it's taken a bit of time—'

'Oh, I wouldn't expect to start high up. Just an ordinary clerical job. At the bottom. You do have clerks, don't you?'

'Yes, but—'

But they were all men. Didn't she know that?

'I'd do *anything*,' the woman said passionately. 'I just want a chance. And then I'd work my way up. I want to be like you, Zeinab.'

'Look,' said Zeinab, 'how old are you?'

The woman flushed.

'Twenty-four,' she muttered. Then, misunderstanding the point, and thinking it was that she was too old, she raised her head defiantly and said:

'I never married. I didn't *want* to get married. Not to the kind of men they suggested. And now I'm too old.'

'Nonsense!' said Zeinab, only just married, at thirty.

'It's true,' the woman insisted. 'And, besides, I—I put men off. I frighten them. I think differently from them. I'm bolder, I think. But they don't want a bold woman. They think a bold woman is just brazen. But I'm not brazen, I just wanted to be different. I wanted to *do* something. Like you, Zeinab. Not just be stuck in a house, cooking my man's meals.'

'I can understand that,' said Zeinab.

The woman glowed.

'Of course you can, Zeinab! And you've found a way out. You've
done it, Zeinab! And I will do it, too. If you will help me.'

'I'm not sure I'm in much of a position to help. I may not be
here much longer. They'll probably want to throw me out.'

'Oh, no, they'd never do that!'

'They're talking of it.'

'The English?'

'No. The Egyptians. And they'll probably want to throw
Cairns-Grant out as well.'

'But he's a great man!'

'Nevertheless.' And then, feeling the need to explain: 'Things
are changing. Egyptians are taking over. Or maybe they're going
to take over. Don't you want that?'

'Oh, yes! Of course, I do, Zeinab. Only—you don't mean
that, do you, Zeinab? About them throwing you out?'

'Yes.'

'But you *are* an Egyptian! Is it—is it because you're a woman,
Zeinab?'

'A lot of men can't get jobs. So they don't like it when they see
a woman doing one. They think it's their job that she's doing.'

'That's it! That's it! And that's what has got to change. And
you'll change it, Zeinab! You've changed it already. And you've
got to go on. You mustn't let them throw you out.'

'Well, it's not as easy as that. In the end I don't have much
say in the matter.'

'If I was beside you, Zeinab, I'd support you. I'd fight for the
things you fight for!'

Zeinab was not much older than she was but felt about a
hundred years older.

'Look,' she said, 'I'm very sorry, but I don't think I'll be able
to help you.'

'I'd wash the floors.'

'We've got men washing the floors. And, anyway, that's not
the level we want women to be working at.'

'Oh, Zeinab, you're so right!'

Zeinab could have bitten her tongue off.

She got up to show her out.

'I can type,' the girl said diffidently. 'I taught myself.'

Zeinab stopped.

'Can you now?'

Perhaps she could do other office things, too. The bane of Zeinab's life were the forms she had to fill in. They were the bane of Cairns-Grant's life, too, and he had delegated them all to Zeinab. She had processed them honourably and diligently, but that was really not her sort of thing. She was miles too impatient.

'Can you now?' she said thoughtfully.

◇◇◇

'No,' said Cairns-Grant. 'It would make things even more difficult and they're difficult enough as it is. They're even objecting to you, Zeinab.'

'Would one more make that much difference?'

'Zeinab, sometimes these days I get really worried. People are so—so crazy! I sometimes think they might aim at the hospital, send us a bomb or something. Just because we employ a woman. Or, of course, an Englishman. I sometimes think I should step down and let an Egyptian have a go. The trouble is there aren't any Egyptian specialists ready in my area. There's Fahmi, of course, and he'll be very good. But not just yet. And there's Rahel. He's training abroad and when he's finished he might well be able to. But not just at the moment. All our training programmes were disrupted by the War.

'But, of course, in your case there's no specialisation involved. In principle a man could do your job. I don't, actually, think he could do it half so well. But that's what they'll say. Are saying. And, anyway, a hospital manager's job *is* specialised. Those bloody forms—'

'Well, actually, it's just there that she might be able to help—'

It was a powerful argument and Cairns-Grant agreed to think about it.

◇◇◇

Meanwhile, though, it might be best to look around. Perhaps there was another area where a lively woman might be employed.

'No,' said Owen flatly. 'They'd go mad. A woman in the Mamur Zapt's office. You know what they'd say?'

'What would they say?'

'That my motives were not strictly honourable. The Mamur Zapt's harem! I can hear it already.'

'You could tough it out. You're always saying that's often the best thing to do.'

'Look, there are a lot of changes—'

'Yes, that's why I thought you might be able to get away with it.'

'These days they're cutting budgets. They're even asking me to reduce staff. And I've only got three! What do you want me to do? Sack Nikos? Or Georgiades?'

◇◇◇

In the end Cairns-Grant came up with a solution.

'A temporary post,' he said. 'To help with an anticipated increase of clerical work. Arising out of the winding down of the military patient programme. Don't want to employ a man since the job would be only temporary. It wouldn't be fair to him. Whereas a woman…'

So it was agreed Miriam should start as a clerk in Zeinab's office.

◇◇◇

And meanwhile the unrest on the streets went on. The students were still marching and still breaking windows. They broke the windows of the big Western shops, their stones rattled against the shutters of the Government offices. The High Commissioner's became a favourite target. The great European hotels, the Savoy, Shepheard's, the Continentale, Mena Palace, and the Semiramis, had all taken to posting armed guards. Europeans began to keep off the streets. Soldiers off duty were confined to bar-

racks, which didn't please them. Some of them slipped out and
went to their usual haunts. On their way back to the barracks,
totally incapable, several of them were beaten up. Whereupon
some of their mates slipped out the next night and responded
in kind, unfortunately rather indiscriminately, which raised the
temperature yet more.

At the Sporting Club people began to mutter. What was
the High Commissioner doing? The Police? The Mamur Zapt?
What were these guys paid for? Send in the Army! They would
know what to do.

'That would only make it worse,' said Owen, at a small meeting he attended at the High Commissioner's.

Garvin, the tough nut who was Head of the Cairo Police,
nodded in agreement.

'We stand ready,' said the Commander in Chief of the Army.

'Well, just stand a bit longer,' said Willoughby.

Nevertheless, he had to do something. What he did was to
arrest Zaghlul, who had made the mistake of leading one of the
processions in person, and deport him to Malta.

'That will show them!' said the Sporting Club members,
pleased.

It did; and the protests in the streets intensified.

◇◇◇

Owen consulted with Paul about getting Mahmoud assigned
to the case.

'Not a chance!' said Paul. 'He's known as a Zaghlul man.
Rushdi Pasha wouldn't have it, the Khedive wouldn't have it—'

He stopped.

'Wait a minute. That could actually help. It would show that
everyone, Wafd as well as the Government, were united in the
desire to track down the perpetrators of this ghastly outrage.
Leave it to me.'

◇◇◇

The Khedive turned the request down flat.

'I would as soon harbour a viper within my bosom—'

'I know exactly how you feel, Your Highness,' said Paul, 'and I'm with you all the way. I think you're very brave.'

'Brave?' said His Highness.

'Yes, to set your face so resolutely against something which could make all the difference to your safety.'

'Just a minute—' said the Khedive.

'Mr. el Zaki is one of the Parquet's ablest men. Not to use him, in the present circumstances, seems, well, a bold decision.'

'Not so fast!' said the Khedive. 'Perhaps, after all…'

Chapter Four

Owen went out to Helwan to see the races. He had not done that before and after an hour or two he decided that he was unlikely to do it again. He was sitting in some raised seats and every so often a few cars whizzed past with a roar of engine and in a cloud of dust and disappeared into the distance. It took just a couple of seconds and that was it; until after a while they stopped going round and one of them was pronounced the winner.

For most of the time, of course, no cars were going past and in the intervals he attempted conversation with his neighbours. This was not easy. For the most part they were the scions of rich families, or else the hangers-on of the scions of rich families, with whom he had little in common. And then the only thing they could talk about was cars, about which Owen knew slightly less than nothing.

'Who do you favour?' one of them asked him.

Owen cast around.

Then, luckily, remembering Zeid's reporting of the boy's comments, he said:

'The De Dion, I think. Or, perhaps, the Brazier.'

This seemed to satisfy the man.

'The Brazier, I think,' he said, and then embarked on a long, incomprehensible disquisition on the merits of the rival engines.

The boy was actually there today. They had seen him as they had driven in. How he had got there Owen couldn't imagine but he went, he said, to most of the races. His name was Salah and he aspired to be a mechanic. He took them over to the start where various cars were lined up, bonnets open, being prepared for their races. Over everything hung the heavy smell of petrol fumes and Owen, not used to them, found his head swimming. He left Zeid with Salah and walked back to the start.

A circuit had been laid out on the desert. The sand was thin and hard and although the track was bumpy at various points, it was relatively flat. Further out into the desert the ground became stonier, so the track was fashioned in the form of an oval. The cars roared off, disappeared, and then roared back again, briefly.

At the furthest point of the circuit the track shimmered. It may have been the petrol fumes or perhaps it was, as it usually was in Egypt, the effects of a mirage. Spirals of heat rose from the ground and shook themselves momentarily into a composed surface, and in that surface there would sometimes appear reflections, as in a mirror: The desert itself, and once some palm trees, and then, astonishingly and very clearly, a vision of cars drawn up, every detail about them as sharp as if they had been standing in front of him.

The heat out there in the desert was quite unbearable; and yet the event had attracted a crowd of onlookers. They crouched in the sand beside the seats and when the cars went past they jumped to their feet and cheered excitedly. Each time the cars circled they drew nearer and nearer to the track until they were almost standing on the track itself. He saw McPhee there, trying to make them get back.

What McPhee was doing there, either, he did not know. A police presence in case of accidents? Crowd control—with a crowd as small as this?

How had he got here, anyway? Not on the donkey he usually rode about Cairo, that was clear. Perhaps Garvin, the police Commandant, whom he had seen somewhere in the crowd, had given him a lift. In his car. Owen felt a little stab of envy. Garvin's car was permanent, Owen's temporary, loaned to him for a few weeks.

The cars were coming round again. There was an awkward bend, sharper than you thought, as the circuit straightened out to go in front of the stands and you could hear the cars before you saw them.

Suddenly there were shouts. Someone had run out on to the track and was standing there waving and gesticulating.

The driver of the first car, some way in front of the others, tried to avoid him and lost control. The car veered off the track into the spectators, spun out again, and lay broad-side across the track, where it stopped. Spectators ran over to it.

And now there were alarmed cries: the other cars were coming.

'Get back! Get back!' shouted Owen, leaping to his feet.

He saw Garvin running forward.

And then, suddenly, there was McPhee, on the track beyond them, waving some coloured material, a shirt, perhaps, ripped off someone's back.

Miraculously the drivers saw him. They were unable to stop, but turned off into the desert and ran past him and the stationary car and the mass of people.

The people were not all round the car. Some of them were round the man who had originally run out on to the track. They were beating him up.

Garvin, already busy with the injured, looked up and saw Owen. He pointed to the man at the centre of the mob.

'Get him away!' he shouted. 'Get him away before they kill him!'

Owen shouldered in, grabbed hold of the man, and pulled him out.

Where could he take him?

He saw his driver and shouted to him: 'Get the car!'

The driver was already running.

Some of the mob had run after Owen and were still striking at the man, and at him.

Suddenly Zeid was there, beating off the blows, forcing away the men.

The boy was there, too, open-mouthed.

Zeid caught Owen's eye and pointed.

His car was coming towards him with a speed at least equal to that the cars had shown on the track.

Owen hustled his captive into a seat. Zeid piled in on top of him. With a roar of its engine the car began to pull away, people still beating at its sides.

'Are you okay?' said Zeid, looking over the back of the car to where the boy was clinging.

Owen got the car to drive over to the other side of the circuit. They all got out.

'What the hell do you think you were doing?' he said to the man.

He wasn't really a man, just a boy. He might even have been a student. He was weeping.

'That was not what I meant!' he sobbed. 'Not what I meant at all!'

'What *did* you mean?'

'I wanted to stop the cars. They are a blasphemy and an abomination. You bring them over here. But we don't want them and we don't want you.'

'Have you seen cars before? You could have got yourself killed.'

'I wouldn't mind being killed,' said the boy defiantly.

'Indeed, you may have killed others.'

The boy began to weep again.

'That was not what I meant!' He rocked to and fro. 'As God is my witness! That was not what I meant at all. I meant only to strike a blow.'

'Against whom?'

'The English,' the boy said. 'All those who bring wicked things to Egypt.'

Zeid touched his forehead.

'He's *magnoum*,' he said. Crazy.

'What are you going to do with him, sir?' asked the driver.

'Take him back to the Bab-el-Khalk. Let Garvin handle this.'

If no one had been hurt, he would probably let him go. If anyone had been injured or killed, however, he would pay the price. Any penalty the courts might impose seemed, though, a little beside the point.

'He's a nutter, sir,' said the driver, starting up the engine.

Maybe.

'Were you alone in this?' he asked.

'Alone.'

'Did you speak to your Sheikh?'

The boy seemed startled.

'I always speak to my Sheikh,' he said. 'He is a holy man.'

'Did you speak to him on this?'

The boy closed his lips firmly.

He might well have done, but probably only in generalities. And it was probably only in generalities that the sheikh had answered him. There were two sorts of sheikh. There was the local chief, to whom people, particularly out in the countryside, owed allegiance; and there was the religious leader, these days, out in the villages, likely to be elderly and set in his ways. He offered some sort of guidance to the village youngsters but it didn't take them far when they moved to the town, as so many of them did now. In the city they lost their bearings and, with their background religiosity, which was the only scheme of values they had, they were easy prey for the radical speakers who knew how to fan simple religion into simple politics.

Yet they weren't all like that. The other boy, Salah, for instance, still perched precariously at the rear of the car, who wanted to be a mechanic, was someone who appeared to have no problem about embracing the modern world, or at any rate, its technology.

'Did you see the De Dion?' he asked Zeid.

'I think so,' said Zeid. He looked back at Salah. 'He said it was.'

'It *was* a De Dion,' the boy called from the back. 'But it didn't look like the same one. The one here was a racer. The other one was a tourer. Modified,' he explained.

'Modified?'

'To make it suitable for ordinary use. The racer is stripped down and powered up. The other one is built up to make it more comfortable. More seating, luggage space, that sort of thing. But it still looks like a racer. To some people,' he added disdainfully.

'So this isn't the one we're interested in?'

'Not unless it's been very stripped down. Of course, he might have two of them. Once you're a De Dion man, you're a De Dion man.'

'Wouldn't that be very expensive?'

'Oh, incredibly,' said Salah.

◇◇◇

Zeinab's would-be helper, Miriam, had not yet, however, cleared all the hurdles in her advance to office. There was still her family to be considered. In practice, this meant her brother, who had become head of the family after the death of her father.

Their father had worked all his life in a humble capacity at the Abdin Palace. That meant there was always money coming in; not much, but enough for him to be able to send his son to college and to give Miriam something of an education at a good school. The family had never been rich, just not badly off, but the father's job had had one great benefit; it had enabled him to plug into a useful system of patronage. Through his Palace connections the father had been able to find his son a job at the Palace, a lowly one, it is true, but nevertheless a job.

Patronage might get you a job but you still needed brains to get on. These Miriam's brother had and he had risen quite quickly to achieve the position of Deputy Controller of the Household. He was able now to live in some style, and the style was Western. He was Western in his clothes—he always wore a neat dark suit—and in his habits. He often went out in the evenings to a club and sometimes to the theatre. And his friends were as often European as they were Egyptian. He had acquired something of a name for introducing Western practice into the Household's accountancy.

This did not, however, mean that he was at all in favour of his sister adopting Western practice, too. She was younger than he was and he had never really thought much about her. On the whole he had assumed that she would be much like their mother and do as she had done; that was, stay at home and mind the house.

When, therefore, Miriam had put her plans to him he had been—well, yes, quite shocked, and had dismissed them on the spot, putting his foot down, in her view, quite brutally. This had only stiffened her resolve. He had found, to his surprise, that she did not take the words he had uttered as the last words on the subject. She had argued back and gone on arguing.

He had found this rather difficult. He wasn't used to argument in the family; in fact, he wasn't used to dissent at all. He had never much noticed her before. He supposed he loved her in a vague, unnoticing kind of way. He had never quite realised how old she was getting. Twenty-three, was it? Twenty-four? She really ought to have been married by now. In fact, she ought to have got married years ago—fifteen was the age when quite a lot of women got married.

His heart smote him. This was bad. He really ought to have done something about it. It was his charge and he had neglected it. There had been so many things to take responsibility for when his father had died and somehow, among them all, he had neglected her. And now, good heavens, she had missed her chance. It was his fault. He was to blame.

So now, when she started talking about what she was going to do with her life, he felt himself in, really, rather a quandary. She was quite right. She had to do something. And marriage now—! But was it *quite* out of the question? He would have to pay, and probably a lot, that was clear. But it was his fault, he should have thought of it earlier, so maybe it was right that he

should. It would still take a bit of negotiation, though, and that
would take time, which was the one thing he was short of...

But this rubbish about going to work in an office, that really
was nonsense! What did she think she was going to do? What
could she do? Had she asked herself that?

Typing. He was taken aback. He hadn't known she could
type. When had she learned that? Had she gone to one of those
places where they specialised in that sort of thing? A business
school? But they were for men. Surely she had not been—

He really had not been performing his duties! He must take
himself in hand, he told himself sternly. It was all very well
concentrating on his work but there were other things too. His
family—had he done enough about them? What would his
father have said? Care for the family was his sacred duty and he
had let it slip.

She had taught herself? She hadn't gone anywhere? Well, that
was a relief! At least she had not made an exhibition of herself
in public. Even so, typing! What might that lead to? He must
put his foot down. He would put it to her clearly...

But still she went on arguing! She wasn't accepting what he
said, and this too, was wrong. He was the head of the household
now and what he said, went.

But it didn't.

The fact was, she had been badly brought up.

But who had been responsible for bringing her up? He had!

She would be working, she said, for a woman. Well, that was
something. But then another thought: how could that be? How
could there be a woman in a position to have others working
for her? A Pasha's daughter? Well, that, too, was something.
But, wait a minute, the Pasha was that old reprobate, Nuri. He
wasn't going to let her have anything to do with him, not on any
account. He wouldn't let her even set foot in his house—

She wasn't going to set foot in his house. She was going to
be working at the hospital.

And so it went on. To everything he said she found an
answer.

His head was in a whirl. How had it come to this? It had got to this because he had not been giving sufficient attention. Well, he would put that right. He would put that right immediately.

What she needed was a bit of discipline. He knew what some of his colleagues would say. A good beating, that's what she needs, they would say.

But somehow he shrank from that. One thing his father had given him was a strong sense of justice. Justice was what moved him most, he often said to his friends. It was, after all, what had led him to involve himself in those things three years ago. And it would not be just to beat his sister for what was really his fault.

Besides, when he had hinted, even just hinted that this could be what her intransigence might lead to, she had flown off the handle completely. Just try it, she had said! You lift a finger against me and I shall walk out!

'Where to?' he had said derisively.

'I'll find a flat,' she had said. 'Don't forget they'll be paying me.'

The very thought was enough to send his brain reeling. What *would* his father say? He had left him the family as his sacred trust and now the family was collapsing. To have a sister leave the family home and set up on her own was unthinkable, quite unthinkable! How would he be able to face his friends, his colleagues? How would he be able to walk down the street?

All right, he was much to blame, but how could she even think of doing something like that? What had got into her? His mother had been too soft with her. What she needed was, yes, a bit of discipline. Her head was full of fantasies. She needed to have them driven out.

And then the thought came to him. Was not that exactly what would happen when she went to this office of hers? He knew about work and the workplace. They wouldn't put up with any nonsense from her. Wouldn't they do it for him? Knock some sense into her head? Not actually beat her, no, they wouldn't do that and that was not what he wanted. But they wouldn't tolerate any of her nonsense and would send her packing. She

would come running home with her tail between her legs. And
then she might be prepared to listen to him. She might even
be willing to let him fix up a marriage for her. That would be
the best solution and maybe this job would bring her round to
seeing that.

◇◇◇

Owen had a new man on the case, or, rather, not a man but
a boy: the boy, Salah. When they had got back to the Bab-el-
Khalk he had taken Salah aside and offered him a huge sum to
come and work for him. Not too huge, actually, for it was the
equivalent of two pints of beer a week. But to Salah it was huge
and it would mean, moreover, that he was staying close to his
beloved cars.

His task was to find out who owned the De Dion that had
brought the 'strangers' to the Water Depot. Owen thought
he would be better at this than Georgiades or Zeid since they
couldn't tell one car from another except by its colour. Besides, a
boy would attract less attention than a man—there were always
lots of boys hanging around in Cairo—and would be able to
worm himself in through the back entrances of the Automobile
Club and the Palace in ways that they could not.

◇◇◇

Mahmoud el Zaki, too, had now been formally assigned to the
case and was familiarising himself with its details in his usual
thorough way. He had been to the Sharia Nubar Pasha and to
the barracks to study the bomb. He had not yet interviewed
Ahmet and Hussein, the drivers of the water-cart, but he and
Owen had worked out a strategy which might enable them to
do so with better profit.

◇◇◇

Owen took Zeid with him down to the Water Depot. They
parted company. Zeid went off to drink tea with the water-cart
drivers, who were just coming back from their morning shift.
Most of the carts had returned now and their drivers had gone

over to lie in the shade of the office building. Owen went in to
see Babikr, the Depot Manager. After a while they emerged and
stood for a moment chatting in the shade.

'You see,' Owen said to the Depot Manager. 'They could have
put other people in danger as well. Your men, for instance.'

'My men?'

Owen stepped close to Babikr and lowered his voice; but not
to the extent that the drivers lying nearest them in the shade
could not hear.

'Yes,' he said. 'We've had a good look at the bomb now. It's
a bit of an amateur contraption and could have gone off at any
time. Even here.'

'Here?' said the Depot Manager.

'Yes. Because that's where it was put in the cart.'

'They couldn't have known!' said Babikr positively.

'Well—'

'You don't mean that they did know?'

'I am afraid they did know. They've told me.'

'Who would have believed it! Ahmet and Hussein! But perhaps—' clutching at straws '—they did not know what it was?'

'I am afraid they did. You see, just before they ran from the
cart, they had done something under it. Primed it so that it
could explode.'

'May God forgive them!'

'It wouldn't have been just the Khedive who was killed if it
had gone off. It would have been the people standing nearby.
Women, children—'

The Depot Manager looked distressed.

'Who could have believed it?' he said, shaking his head.
'Ahmet and Hussein!'

'Yes, I know, I was surprised, too. But what makes it worse,
you see, is that it could have gone off here. The people they
worked with. Their mates!'

'I cannot believe… But perhaps it wouldn't have gone off?
They hadn't primed it?'

'We-ll, as I told you it was a bit of a contraption. Not an expert job. It could have gone off at any time.'

'But perhaps they didn't know that?'

'Someone did. The person who made it.'

'But that wouldn't have been Ahmet and Hussein—'

'No. But it was in their cart. And the people who put it there must have been told what to do. And how to set it up. It had to be done very carefully.'

'But perhaps that was not Ahmet and Hussein?'

'Who was it, then?'

'Someone must have come in.'

'When?'

'At night.'

'Is there no watchman?'

'Of course there is. And the place is kept locked.'

'Perhaps the watchman was sleeping.'

'But Ali's a good man! He wouldn't have—'

'There is another thing: suppose men had come in at night. In the dark. How would they have known which was the cart to put it in? Dozens of carts? All in rows? All exactly alike? Does it not *have* to have been Ahmet and Hussein?'

The Depot Manager was silent.

'Or,' said Owen, 'one of the other men who work here?'

◇◇◇

The watchman lived in a ramshackle hut on the edge of the Depot. When they got there, he was out. He had gone down to the river, said his aged wife, to fetch water.

'And what's wrong with that?' she asked fiercely. 'How else am I going to do my cooking?'

'Nothing's wrong with that, Mother,' said Owen hastily.

'I know what you're thinking. You're thinking: why does the man have to do that while the woman sits on her ass at home?'

'No, no—'

'I'll tell you why. Because I've got a bad back, that's why!'

'It's all right, no one—'

'I can't sleep at night. Not with my back. And if I can't sleep, of course, neither can he. He has to get out of bed and wander round. Well, that's his job, isn't it? That's what he ought to be doing. He can sleep in the day time. When I'm making his meal.' She cackled. 'Mind you, there was a time when he wasn't so keen to get out of bed! He was younger then and had better things to do.'

She nudged Owen.

'Better things to do,' she repeated.

'Yes, yes.'

'He was all right *then*. And so was I. Mind you, I paid for it. Five children we've got. And that did for my back. So it's only right that he should fetch the water.'

They could see the watchman hobbling up from the river. He put down the heavy wooden bucket he was carrying.

'Come on, come on!' cried the old woman impatiently. 'The Effendi's waiting for you. And so am I.'

He put the bucket down in front of her. She seized it and bore it off inside.

'You see that?' grumbled the old man. 'She can carry it if she wants to! There's nothing wrong with her back now!'

'What's that?' called the old woman.

'I said you keep very well for your age.'

'So I do, so I do. But what's that got to do with the Effendi? He doesn't want to know that, does he?'

'Yappety-yap,' complained the watchman. 'All day! And all night, too,' he added, under his breath.

'She drives you out, I gather,' said Owen, smiling.

'I go down by the river,' said the watchman. 'It's quieter there.'

'Can you see the carts from there? In the dark?'

'It's not been dark lately. There's been good moonlight. And in any case,' he said, 'that's not what I go by.'

'What do you go by?'

The old man pulled his ear.

'These. I may not see so well these days but I can hear a bat squeak.'

Owen asked him if he had been aware of anyone coming into the Depot at night recently and interfering with the carts.

The old man said he hadn't. He would, perhaps, have said that anyway, but Owen was inclined to believe him. He thought it unlikely, in any case, that the bomb had been placed in the cart that way.

◇◇◇

Zeid joined him afterwards. As they were walking back to the Bab-el-Khalk together he asked him about the response of the cart men to what they had overheard. Zeid said that it had certainly made an impression on them but that they hadn't said much.

Owen told him to hang around the Depot for the next few days and see if he could pick up anything.

'Lay it on that the bomb could have gone off in the Depot,' he said. 'In which case some of them might well no longer be here. What sort of bastard could have done a thing like that? That sort of thing. Ask them if anyone had seen Ahmet or Hussein bringing a package in. Or anyone else. Did Ahmet and Hussein have enemies?'

'It may take a bit of time,' Zeid warned. 'They'll have to get used to me.'

'Tell them that it's nicer here than in the station at the moment. Say that everyone is running round in circles because it's the Khedive. You want to keep out of it. In any case, you don't care tuppence about the Khedive. What you can't get over, though, is that anyone could do this to their mates.'

'I get the picture,' said Zeid.

◇◇◇

Over to their left the hawks were still circling. It looked to be in the same place. Clearly the new drop of refuse had not yet been picked dry.

The hawks did not land. They circled, and then dipped in and seized what had caught their eye and then flew off again.

Consumed, as some of the shops selling liquor said in a large notice displayed on the door or in the window, off the premises.

The hawks in Cairo were a protected bird. They were scavengers and kept the streets clean. Or so the Health Department said. If this was true, how was it that the streets were so dirty?

They were allowed to proliferate, and then, when they became too numerous and over-intrusive, there would be a cull. This was made easier by the behaviour of the hawks when one of them was killed. The other hawks would gather round, flying in on the dead bird and touching it with their wings. Sometimes, if you were standing by, they would mob you. The police would shoot one and then, when the others came, shoot the others. The police always enjoyed the occasion. It was good practice.

Chapter Five

With Mahmoud's formal assignment to the case, the status of the investigation altered. It was now not a security matter but a legal investigation which could lead to prosecution. It was Mahmoud's job, as the responsible officer of the Parquet, to examine the evidence, decide whether it should lead to prosecution, and then present the case in court. His role, therefore, included, as in the French system on which the Egyptian system was based, both investigation and prosecution. If he decided that there wasn't a case to answer, then that was that.

Mahmoud felt comfortable with this. He was not at all happy about the Mamur Zapt having powers which bordered on the extra-judicial. There was nothing personal in this. He and Owen were close friends. In fact, Owen was probably his only close friend. Mahmoud had had to work his way up and on the way he had been too busy to make friends. (Enemies, possibly, but not friends.) His objection to the position of Mamur Zapt was a legal one. There was, or should be, no place for such a role in a modern legal system.

This was not even a question of British usurpation of the role, although that was certainly how he saw it. The position was a hangover from the days of the Ottoman Empire. The Mamur Zapt was directly appointed by the Khedive and responsible only to him. Mahmoud didn't like this. It smacked too much of the old days and of the practices which Mahmoud was anxious to reform. So he was both pleased and relieved to have taken things over; pleased to get out from behind that dead-end desk, relieved that at last things could be done properly. Mahmoud liked things to be done properly. None of this English fudging and shifting and compromising!

Owen, too, was happy to work this way. It was consistent, he thought, with the way the British Administrator should operate: behind the scenes, letting the Egyptians run the system until one day they could take it over entirely. Condescending, perhaps, but pragmatic. For Owen the world was not necessarily just or fair or even rational; it just had to be made to work. So he was quite content to take a formal back seat in the investigation. Investigation was only incidentally his job. His job, certainly at the moment, was to see that things didn't boil over. That was what the Khedive had appointed him for, and it chimed in quite well with the way the British saw the role.

In practice, Owen and Mahmoud worked well together. They might disagree over principle and politics, but on day-to-day matters they usually saw eye-to-eye.

◇◇◇

Mahmoud decided to question the prisoners: this despite Mr. Narwat's warning that he would instruct them to say nothing.

'In their interests,' he said.

Mahmoud nodded, and went ahead.

'You are Hussein Farbi?' he said.

Hussein looked at Mr. Narwat. Mr. Narwat nodded.

'Yes,' said Hussein.

'And you are a driver on a water-cart?'

Hussein looked at Mr. Narwat. Mr. Narwat hesitated.

'No matter,' said Mahmoud. 'There is unlikely to be disagreement over this in court. And you were watering the road ahead of the Royal Procession?'

'Perhaps you shouldn't answer this,' instructed Mr. Narwat.

Mahmoud shrugged.

'I don't think there's going to be much disagreement over that either,' he said.

'Course I was,' said Hussein. 'Everyone knows that!'

'And the cart broke down?'

'There is no need to answer that question,' said Mr. Narwat.

'Why shouldn't I answer it?' asked Hussein. 'That's what happened.'

Mr. Narwat shrugged.

'So it broke down?'

'Yes.'

'Why? Have you an idea?'

'The pin came out.'

'Ah, you felt the wheel coming loose?'

'That's right.'

'So that's why you stopped?'

'Of course.'

'And jumped down and had a look under the cart?'

'You shouldn't answer that question,' said Mr. Narwat.

Hussein looked puzzled, then shrugged. He didn't answer.

'Did you see the bomb?'

'Don't answer!' warned Mr. Narwat.

Hussein shrugged again.

'Then why did you run away?' asked Mahmoud.

'Don't—' began Mr. Narwat.

'I didn't run away!' protested Hussein.

Mahmoud laughed.

'There are more than a hundred people who will say that you did,' he said.

Hussein looked confused.

'Just keep your mouth shut!' snapped Mr. Narwat. 'In your own interests!'

'I wonder if it *is* in his interests?' said Mahmoud as if considering the matter.

'Of course it is!' said Mr. Narwat sharply.

Mahmoud shrugged.

'Your decision,' he said. 'But if he was my client I would be wondering whether it was wise for him to shoulder responsibility for the incident when it is quite clear that someone else has put him up to it.'

◇◇◇

'My client,' said Mr. Narwat, 'is saying nothing.'

And, indeed, Ahmet was saying nothing. He closed his lips firmly and couldn't be persuaded even into admitting that his name was Ahmet.

Mr. Narwat, who had put his finger to his lips when Ahmet came in and scowled fiercely, could be proud of him.

Mahmoud did not seem bothered. He nodded every time Ahmet refused to answer and wrote something down on the pad he had with him. After several minutes of this he said:

'Right, let me make sure I've got this right.'

He read out the list of questions he had put and at the end of each one said: 'Accused refused to answer.'

'Not *refused*,' interjected Mr. Narwat. '"Chose." Chose not to answer.'

He looked at Mahmoud and Owen triumphantly.

'Not "refused,"' wrote Mahmoud obediently. '"Chose." Accused chose not to answer.' Oh, and one other question I did not include in my list. '"Asked why he had run away from the water-cart, the accused chose not to answer."'

'I am not entirely happy about the way you are presenting this,' said Mr. Narwat.

'Have I not reported it correctly?'

'You have reported it correctly so far as it goes,' said Mr. Narwat. 'But you have not left open the possibility that my client may deny that he ran away.'

'He did not say that,' said Mahmoud. 'I am reporting only what he said or did not say. I will note your objection if you wish.'

'No need,' said Mr. Narwat.

'And can I clarify one point? Witnesses say that while both men climbed down off the cart, one of them climbed down first and looked under the cart. Which one of you was that?'

'Say nothing!' ordered Mr. Narwat.

'I am just trying to clarify the points because it could make a difference to charging. Mr. Farbi claims that he was the one who looked under the cart. I just wanted to know if your client disputes this?'

Mr. Narwat rubbed his chin.

'I don't see why he should,' he said.

'No, I don't, either. But I just wanted to get it straight. In case it could affect the charging.'

'Why should if affect the charging?'

'Because I am adding a charge to the ones Captain Owen read out previously. If you will allow me a moment, I will just get the wording right; but it will be to the effect that your clients knowingly sought to cause an explosion in the Sharia Nubar Pasha with the intention of killing the Khedive.'

'Knowingly?' said Mr. Narwat.

'Yes, knowingly. And, on reflection, I think it can safely be applied to both of them.'

◇◇◇

'Knowingly?' asked Owen, after Ahmet had been returned to the cells and Mr. Narwat had departed.

'Yes. They primed the bomb before running away and I don't see how that could be done other than knowingly. The mixture is exploded when the nitric acid runs into the picric. That happens when the small bottle of nitric acid inside the lip is tilted. That's what they did before running away. It can be done only at the last moment. My guess is that's what Hussein was doing when he looked under the cart the last time, in the Nubar Pasha. The cotton wool packed into the top of the bottle is just to slow the whole thing down and give them time to get away.'

'Georgiades was lucky, then.'

'Yes. Perhaps the cotton wool was stuffed in too tightly.'

'I'm surprised. I didn't think Hussein and Ahmet were like that.'

'I didn't think they were like that, either. I thought they were just ordinary cart drivers persuaded into it by money. But if they were prepared to go as far as they did, there must be more to them. I think we'll need to look into them more closely.'

◇◇◇

Outside, in the street, the heat had built up. Fortunately, for the first part of the journey, he could cut through the park and be under the shade of some trees. There were casuarina trees and gnarled pepper trees, bohinia trees with their porcelain pink blossoms and pods which the parakeets loved. The parakeets had been let out of the Giza Zoo years before and thriven in the parks.

There were other birds, too: warblers and bee-eaters, hoopoes with their gold crests, weaver birds weaving their little round ball-like nests, palm doves gurgling in the palms, and, of course, crows and kite hawks everywhere. Between the crows and the kites there was constant warfare. They fought for every scrap of food. When they found it, though, they behaved differently. The hawks zoomed away with it, whereas the crows, the Cairo crows, anyway, would bury it, planting it in a flower bed and then covering it with leaves. Over beyond the end of the gardens hawks were circling, so he knew he was going in the right direction.

He came out near the hammam in Shafik Street. Long before he got there he could smell the refuse heap beside it. He wondered if the smell penetrated the baths? Through the vents, perhaps? Maybe they were used to it.

He had hoped to intercept Georgiades somewhere around here. The Greek had been retracing the route taken by the water-cart from the Depot to the Sharia Nubar Pasha. It had been easy to find out the route, all the drivers knew it: but it was a rather different thing to find out from people along the way whether they had seen the cart on the morning of the Procession. It was a long shot, Owen knew, but it was worth a try. He couldn't believe that Hussein and Ahmet had carried the bomb into the Depot and fixed it beneath the cart under the eyes of all the other drivers. Possibly, just possibly, it had been brought in during the night, and if it was Hussein and Ahmet who had done the fixing, they would know the right cart. But would they have risked it, with the watchman, sleepless because of his wife, wandering around? No, more likely it had been done as they were on their way to the Sharia Nubar Pasha.

Georgiades came into view, walking slowly and pausing frequently to mop his face because of the heat. Whenever he stopped he turned his large, brown, sympathetic eyes on people and invited commiseration—and confidences. It was hard to resist Georgiades. Old ladies, old men on their donkeys, shop-keepers taking the air, stall holders packing up for the siesta, all were drawn into conversation.

Owen looked round for a café and found a small one with two tables outside. He sat down at one of the tables and then, as Georgiades came up, waved to him to join him.

'It's very hot,' the Greek complained. 'I'm sweating like a pig. You know, I think I might even go into the hammam.'

'Well, don't take too long,' said Owen. 'You're only half way.'

'Especially as the cart stopped there that morning.'

'Really?' Owen looked at him quickly. 'Well, neither of them would have been wanting a bath.'

'Do you know,' said Georgiades, 'that's exactly what someone else said. And why they noticed it.'

'Did they go in?'

'Yes.'

'And pick up anything?'

'That's what I was hoping to find out.'

◇◇◇

Owen decided not to wait. Georgiades, if he knew his man, would make the most of this opportunity to escape the Cairo heat. He would probably stay in the hammam for hours. He might well emerge with something which would make it useful but it could be a long time to wait. Besides, sitting outside at a table, the smell of the refuse was overwhelming.

Here the battle between the hawks and the crows had resulted in a victory for the hawks. There were very few crows in evidence, not enough for the hawks even to mount a challenge.

They circled overhead keeping a watchful eye on the situation and occasionally swooping down for some tid-bit. Victory in this as in most battles—Owen, who had done some soldiering in India before he came to Egypt, knew his military theory—went to the side which could bring most resources to bear on a certain point, and the hawks had got the advantage here.

Just beyond the refuse dump was a figure Owen recognised: Miss Skiff. She was kneeling down trying to coax a cat to take some food from her hand.

Owen wouldn't have done the same for worlds. The dump crawled with cats, which alternated preying for food with curling up on top of the hammam around the vents, where they could enjoy the continued warmth of the sun and of the steam escaping. They were pretty well all feral, abandoned to run wild, as were most cats in Egypt in Owen's opinion.

'Were you thinking of taking that one home to the Mission, Miss Skiff?'

Miss Skiff rose and dusted her knees.

'Perhaps not,' she said regretfully. 'Although it does seem a shame to leave them here in these disgusting conditions.'

'I think they're rather enjoying them. You don't seek to rescue all animals, then, Miss Skiff?'

'The task would be never ending. So what brings you here, Captain Owen? Not the cats, I fancy.'

'No. I'm still on the trail of that water-cart that concerned us the other day.'

'Ah, yes. The horses.'

'They're safe and sound, I'm sure you'll be glad to know, and back at the Depot. Or, rather, out on the roads again.'

Miss Skiff nodded.

'They like work,' she said. 'It gives them something to do. A task in life. Otherwise they would get bored.'

'And you, too, Miss Skiff, see yourself with a task? You and your ladies?'

'Oh, yes.'

'Always out on the roads?'

'Most days, yes.'

'I wonder—'

'Yes?'

'I wonder if you or they might have noticed a cart?'

'We would have *seen* a cart very probably. We always look out for horses.'

'This one was a special one. It was the one you saw in the Sharia Nubar Pasha.'

'Ah!'

'I wonder if any of you had seen it previously that day.'

'Well, we might have *seen* it, but—'

'Stopping. With men working under it. As if it had broken down.'

'Ah, you want to see if it had broken down before?'

'Yes.'

'Well, we might have seen it but I don't think we would have noticed it unless it was blocking up the traffic or something.'

'Perhaps I should come clean. It's about the bomb. I think it quite likely that it was put in the cart somewhere between the Water Depot and the Sharia Nubar Pasha, and I wondered if any of your ladies might have seen that happening.'

'Well, I will ask, but—'

'It might look as if the cart had broken down and the men were trying to fix it.'

Miss Skiff nodded.

'And then, of course, they would have left lighting the fuse until they got to the Nubar Pasha.'

'It wasn't that kind of bomb.'

'Oh? What kind of bomb was it?'

'Well, it wasn't one where you had to light a fuse. More a question of chemical action.'

'Oh, really?' said Miss Skiff, interested. 'How did that work? Do tell me. I used to be a science teacher.'

'Well, it was a question of releasing nitric acid into picric acid.'

Miss Skiff nodded.

'Oh, yes,' she said. 'I can see how that might work.'

'As a bomb, it has shortcomings. One of them is that it would be unstable.'

'Depends on the arrangements for mixing,' said Miss Skiff.

'What concerns me is that the arrangements were rather gim-crack. The movement of the cart, which is not exactly smooth, could have detonated it prematurely. And then the horses—'

'Yes. I can see about the horses,' said Miss Skiff impatiently. 'But also innocent passers-by. Well, I can see why you want to find out whether the bomb was put in the cart on the way and will make inquiries. But as to stopping—or even taking a pack-age on board—there could be quite an innocent explanation. These carts are always picking up packages and delivering them around the city. It is a sort of unofficial postal service, and very convenient, since the water-carts go everywhere. Ordinary people might well use them instead of the more formal postal service. It's cheaper, for a start—just a few coins to the drivers.'

'You seem to know the city pretty well, Miss Skiff.'

'I *should* know it,' said Miss Skiff. 'I have lived in it for nearly fifty years now.'

◇◇◇

It was early evening by the time Georgiades got back to the Bab-el-Khalk. No, he protested indignantly, he had not spent the whole afternoon in the baths. When he had come out, he had continued to retrace the route the cart had taken, right up to the Sharia Nubar Pasha. This was not as satisfactory, he acknowledged as replicating it in the morning, when the cart had actually made its journey, and he would probably need to do that bit again the next morning; but the people on the route did not change that much and he had been anxious to catch them as soon after the event as he could, while all was still fresh in their minds.

'And did you find out anything in the hammam?'

'Yes.'

A package had definitely been picked up. But exactly when, or where, or from whom it was transferred, Georgiades was not yet able to say. They had not picked it up from Reception, which was where it might have been expected to have been left. The receptionist was adamant that no package had been given to him. It must have been picked up inside. That was quite possible for inside was a series of rooms and something could have been passed at any point. The most likely place was the changing room. Someone could have been waiting there, apparently changing, before or after having a bath, and then simply taken the package out of a locker and passed it to the two men.

Well, not quite so simply. There was usually an attendant in the room. But money could pass as easily as packages, and the m'allim might have been bribed. Or else the package could have been passed while his attention was distracted. He had assured Georgiades that he had not been aware of any transaction of that kind at that time.

Had he been aware of the two men coming in? He might have remembered them because it was probable that they didn't go on in to take the baths but had just entered and left the changing room.

He couldn't swear to that, there had been people coming and going, and there had been a problem about towels. But he thought it possible. People did drift in occasionally to chat to their friends but when they did they usually took a bath as well. The hammam was a great meeting place for people, somewhere where they could sit and chat. It was, said the m'allim, carried away, the hub of the universe.

More mundanely it was also a place where even people like water-cart drivers might drop in, especially if they were doing someone a favour by picking up something to pass on.

A package had, however, definitely been picked up somewhere inside. At the entrance to the hammam had been the usual cluster of beggars and they recalled two men coming out carrying a parcel. They had rushed to offer their services; and they recalled the occasion clearly because of the sharpness with which their offer had been spurned.

◇◇◇

Miriam had been given a desk in a corner of Zeinab's office, behind which she sat surrounded by mountains of unprocessed forms. The fact was that, faced with the flood of military patients, Zeinab had chosen to concentrate on essentials: like seeing that the soldiers got their pay while in hospital (which accorded very much with the priorities of the Australians themselves).

The Army, after some skirmishing, had agreed to send in its pay clerks, but had insisted that the patients parade outside the office assigned them so that the soldiers could be ticked off properly. Apart from the difficulty of getting severely wounded patients out of bed, this had blocked up the corridors. After some battles roughly equivalent in ferocity to those they had been fighting in the desert, the Army agreed that its clerks might go round the beds.

The question then arose of what the patients might do with their money. They knew very well what they wanted to do with it and Zeinab, for perhaps the first time, was glad that the nurses were men. In the end they settled for beer instead but this caused problems too and for a while Zeinab contemplated bringing the military police into the hospital as well as the army clerks. Here, too, though, the patients found that they had overestimated themselves and the problem subsided.

What had not subsided, however, were the mounds of forms that the Army decreed necessary about any of its members lying in bed. Might they be malingering? In which case they should be discharged. Might they be dead? In which case they were improperly being paid. In either case, the situation needed monitoring, and that required forms.

And there the forms were, unfilled in, on Miriam's desk. Zeinab had ignored them.

At the end of the first morning Miriam said tentatively:

'What I think we need is a better way of doing this.'

'Right!' said Zeinab with relief. 'You find it.'

Miriam could actually see some improvements that might be made but felt the need of experience. Her brother, of course, had this in plenty so she put some of the problem to him when he came home that evening. It took some time for him to see that they were engaged in a real conversation here and when he did he was taken aback. No one had ever asked him about methods before and he rather doubted that she could understand what was involved. When she showed that she did he was for the moment nonplussed; but then realised that she must have unconsciously picked up some things from him as she was sitting next to him when he pored over his papers late at night. However, he did his best to explain it at her level.

The next day she came back with more questions. She had tried some of his suggestions and this was what she had found… Ah, well, in that case, then, she should try…

He found her surprisingly quick. It must be a sort of hereditary talent, he thought, although he was surprised to find that it could pass down the female line. Actually, he rather enjoyed explaining things to her. At last here was someone who could appreciate what he was doing. He was drawn to expounding the delights of the new filing system he was introducing. She asked if she could come along and see it in operation.

Here, however, he drew back. This was a step too far. What would they think at the Palace? Bringing a women in? Even his sister. No, no, it was too—

'It seems a pity,' she said. 'Such an interesting system…'

That was true, he thought. And maybe she was right: it probably would work in a hospital. Perhaps, he suggested diffidently, he might come to *her* office and think about what might be made of it. She jumped at the idea.

Afterwards, he chided himself. What he should be doing was arranging a marriage for her, not introducing her to the pleasure of office management. He was merely reinforcing her in her foolishness and, yes, sinfulness. As the head of the family, he was a let down.

◇◇◇

Things were accumulating on Owen's desk, too. Almost every hour reports came in of disturbances here, trouble there. Attacks on people in one place, or property in another. More and more people were getting killed.

Willoughby had thought that getting rid of Zaghlul would end the problem. But it didn't, as Owen could have told him, had tried to tell him. It wasn't just a case of a small group of conspirators, as loud-voiced people of the Sporting Club supposed, it was a much wider expression of feeling.

'What are you doing, Owen?' they said. 'Jump on them!'

'You don't jump on a whole people,' he said.

◇◇◇

Something had to be done about it, of course. The Army was out in force, the police were busy night and day. There were incessant meetings. Garvin was too busy to attend them. He sent his Deputy, McPhee, instead. McPhee couldn't understand any of it. He was an old-timer and what was happening now was completely beyond his grasp. Garvin pleaded with Owen to get to the meetings if he could, to put some sense into them, but Owen himself had plenty to do. And what could he say to them?

'The problem is political,' he kept insisting. 'Not military. Force isn't the answer.'

They thought he'd gone soft.

◇◇◇

Paul Trevelyan hadn't been seen for days. He seemed to be spending all his time on the wire to London. Or Paris, now that the big conference at Versailles had started, and most of the British Government had moved there. At last he emerged, and when Owen went to visit him at his office, he was opening a bottle of champagne.

'Just for you and me,' he said. 'We've done it!'

'Done—?'

'They're sending out a Commission.'

'That's great, Paul!' He raised the glass to his lips. 'But—'

But would it make any difference?

'You've always said the problem was political, not military,' said Paul. 'Now we've got the chance of a political solution.'

He knew Paul expected him to be pleased. And he was, he was. It was just that, in his experience, sending out busybody know-nothings from London usually didn't help at all.

'But will they get anywhere, Paul?' he couldn't help saying.

'Oh, they will,' said Paul confidently. 'With me holding their hands and whispering in their ears. The important thing is to get all interested parties round a table, talking.'

He put his finger on his lips and lowered his voice mock-conspiratorially.

'There's even a chance,' he whispered, 'that I might persuade the Old Man to bring back Zaghlul.'

'That would be great, Paul. That really would!'

He meant it, too. Unless you had everybody in, there wouldn't be a chance of any agreement sticking. He raised his glass.

'To you, Paul!'

'Thanks.'

Paul sipped the champagne.

'And to you, of course,' he said, putting the glass down.

'Me?'

'In anticipation. You're a big part of this, you know.'

'Well, I wouldn't say that—'

'Oh, but you are. They wouldn't have come without you.'

'Sorry?'

'They insisted on absolute security. For the members of the Communion. Wouldn't come without it. Had to give an absolute guarantee. Of course, I said I could. We've got just the man. I said. Bags of experience. Knows Cairo like the back of his hand. If any man can keep them safe, he can.'

'Thank you, Paul. Thank you very much,' said Owen bitterly.

Chapter Six

Owen wanted to take a look at the hammam himself.

He decided to pass himself off as an ordinary user of the baths' services. The hammams were public baths and anyone could use them. And very many people did. They weren't like public baths in European cities. In Europe people had baths in their own houses so public baths were less frequently used, less central to people's lives. In Egypt the houses didn't usually have baths so nearly everyone went to the hammam.

They expected a lot from them. They went there to have their bodies put in order, to be given a good servicing, like cars being checked into a garage. It wasn't just one bath but several, each with a different function. Massage was an integral part of it, even for the humblest user. Soaping and oiling were important. Injuries could be put right, physical weaknesses sympathetically addressed.

But perhaps the most important function of the hammam was the social one. People went there to meet their friends and to catch up on the latest news. The issues of the day were discussed. Public opinion was registered there and possibly formed. It was a good place, then, to take the temperature of the city and Owen thought he would do that as well.

With his dark Welsh colouring it was easy to pass himself off as a Levantine of some kind and his Arabic was certainly sufficient for that. He discarded his usual red Governmental tarboosh in favour of a nondescript one of brown plaid such as an Effendi working in a business house might wear.

As he approached the hammam he checked to see there wasn't a towel over the door. He had taken it for granted from the fact that Georgiades hadn't mentioned it that it was a hammam for men only. But it might not have been. Some hammams were mixed. Men and women went on different days and when there were women inside a towel was draped over the door. Zeinab had told him that the hammam was an important part of the Egyptian marriage market. Mothers went there to inspect the flesh and see that it was suitable for their beloved sons.

From outside, the hammam could be taken for a small mosque, with its facade of red and white stone intermixed, panelled and arabesqued. It could be distinguished by the fact that the hammam's entrance was usually very narrow, rather below the level of the street, and had its door recess painted green.

From the doorway you entered first a tiny space in which a receptionist was sitting. From there you were at once ushered into the meslakh, or reception room, which was always off at an angle so that you couldn't see directly into it from the street. This was because the reception room was also the changing room. It was also a room in which you could lie around and chat. There was an octagonal fountain in the middle of it, encased with white marble, from which there was a fierce, cold jet.

Around the walls were white marble couches with cushions. Some of the couches had handsome gilt screens in front of them to give privacy; behind which, he thought, a package might easily be passed.

The room was arched and domed and from some of the arches cages were hanging containing singing birds. The air was filled with their twittering and warbling.

The m'allim, or keeper of the baths, came up smiling. He had two attendants. One took Owen's shoes, the other his clothes. The m'allim himself took his watch, wallet, and other valuables.

'Suppose I was carrying something big,' said Owen: 'Would you be able to keep it for me?'

'If it was as big as a horse,' said the m'allim confidently.

'And fragile?'

'My hands are as soft as petals, Effendi, and I would store it as in a bed of roses.'

'Thank you. Yes. Well, thank you.'

He was given towels and clogs, since in the harara which he was going to next, the floor was often wet.

The attendant took his shoes and clothes away. The clothes were placed in a locker, which might be big enough to hold a reasonable-sized package, and the shoes placed on a rack below. The m'allim took his valuables and locked them in a special safe-like box.

He wandered on into the harara. The harara was the main room where baths were taken and the body massaged. It was filled with steam and for a moment he stopped because the heat was so overwhelming. Around the room men were lying on marble slabs, as in a mortuary thought Owen, then stilled the thought quickly.

They were being worked on. Attendants in loin-cloths stooped over them, bending, pulling, and twisting this limb and that. From time to time there was a loud crack.

The cracks were particularly frequent, in fact, they seemed a necessary part of it, when they were working on the neck. The head was twisted first this way and then that and each time the neck gave a loud crack.

But that was nothing, thought Owen, compared with what they did to the feet. The soles of the feet were rasped with heavy rasps, like cheese or breadcrumb graters, made from Assouan clay and shaped like crocodiles. He supposed that if you walked barefoot much of the time, or, maybe, in sandals your feet might become so hard that they needed rasping.

He thought he might forego this part and went over to where there were some smaller rooms with tanks of water into which you could plunge. Near the tanks a man was standing with loofah and soap. Owen was seized, soaped and scrubbed, and then had water poured over him. Getting into the tanks was optional. Steam was rising from the tank nearest him and the water appeared to be boiling. As he watched, a pink, lobster-like figure emerged from the bubbles like Venus emerging from the sea. Well, not quite like Venus: it was a short, fat, flabby man, who stood for a moment, gasping, while the attendant poured cold water down his back.

'One of these days,' said the man, 'this is going to do it for me!' Owen thought he would forego that bit, too.

The attendant wrapped them both in towels and they went to the beyt-owwal, where they lay on couches, this time with cushions, drinking coffee and talking. From time to time a lawingi would come in and rub someone's feet or knead their bodies.

Owen asked his neighbour if he came here often.

'Most days,' said the man. He shrugged. He said, that his wife complained he smelt of hilba and that she sent him to the baths to get rid of it.

'You can't,' said a man near him. 'It's inside you.'

Hilba was a strongly smelling, auburn-coloured substance which many Egyptians consumed in large quantities for its alleged curative properties. It dyed their palms red and made their bodies exude a distinct smell. Odeur d'arabe, some of Owen's sniffy Egyptian friends called it, and they shunned it like the plague.

'What's wrong with it?' asked someone.

'Well, she's a Christian, you see,' said Owen's neighbour, 'and doesn't like it.'

'Oh, for goodness sake!' said someone. 'Why don't you get another wife?'

'I was thinking of that. Several of them,' said Owen's neighbour, roaring with laughter.

The men fell to discussing the different smells of people. Armenians, they thought, smelled of pastrami and Italians of camomile. Greeks, they thought, smelled of garlic and brilliantine, and when they sweated, their arm-pits smelled of yoghurt.

Owen hadn't noticed this and made up his mind to check when Georgiades was next in the room. He wondered uneasily what he himself smelled like.

'One thing you can be sure of,' said the m'allim, who had been listening with interest. 'My baths will clean anything. Inside or outside. And afterwards you will be as fragrant as a lily.'

'Now, why hasn't my wife noticed that?' asked Owen's neighbour.

'How do you think the Khedive smells?' asked someone.

'French?' suggested someone.

'Or English.'

They all laughed.

'I'll tell you one thing,' said someone else. 'I'll bet he doesn't smell of hilba!'

They seemed in no hurry to go. Owen remarked as much to the m'allim when he went to collect his valuables.

'Oh, they like to put the world to rights,' said the m'allim.

'There are worse ways to do that,' said Owen, 'than sitting in a hammam talking.'

'That's just what I say!' said the m'allim. 'You'd do better to come here than get up to some of the things you get up to, I say.'

'Ah, but you don't have people like that, do you?'

'You'd be surprised!'

'Oh, by the way,' said Owen, 'a friend of mine was supposed to be passing on something to someone here the other day. You don't know if he did, do you?'

'What was it?' asked the m'allim.

'A parcel, probably.'

'Someone else was asking that.'

'Probably someone else from our office. We're a bit anxious about it and wanted to be certain that it had been passed on.'

'I think someone came for it.'

'Carriers?'

'Yes. Sort of.'

'Water cart, probably?'

'Yes, that's what it was.'

'That's all right, then. As long as it was the parcel we're talking about. You don't remember the person who brought it in, do you?'

'I'm afraid I don't.'

Owen slipped him some money.

'As a matter of fact, I do,' said the m'allim. 'He was an effendi. Like yourself.'

'Young and handsome?' said Owen, smiling.

'Of course.'

'And smelling of hilba?'

'Attar of roses, I think,' said the m'allim.

◇◇◇

Outside, as Georgiades had told him, were the beggar-boys.

'Effendi, Effendi!' they cried, as soon as they saw him. 'Bakhshish!'

Owen stopped.

'Bakhshish,' he said, 'has to be earned.'

'Okay,' said one of the boys resignedly. 'Behind the hammam, then.'

'Not in that way,' said Owen. 'That is a bad way.' He took out a coin and balanced it in his fingers. 'I give this,' he said, 'for information.'

'You want to know who goes to the hammam?'

'That's right. This person came last week. He was an effendi, like me, and was carrying a package.'

'Someone else asked us about the package.'

'That's right. And you told him that you had seen men come out carrying one.'

'That is true, Effendi.'

'What I want to know about is the man who carried it *in*.'

'An effendi, you say?'

'That's right.'

'We didn't really notice him.'

'Like me. And smelling of roses.'

'I think I remember,' said one of the boys.

'What was he like?'

'Richer than you, Effendi.'

'Very probably. But what makes you think so?'

'His clothes, Effendi.'

The boy made a gesture with his hands which somehow conveyed comfort, display, casual affluence.

'And the way he walked,' said another boy.

'How did he walk?'

'As if he didn't see us.' The boy lifted his nose into the air as if he was disregarding a bad smell.

'As if we were ants,' said someone else.

Owen nodded. These were the things they noticed. What in England would be registered as class. In Egypt it wasn't quite class but a different kind of superiority.

They gave him a description of the man's face, too, but there was nothing that made it different from any other face. What had stood out for them, and what they kept returning to, was the assumption of superiority. It wasn't just that he was a nas taibene, a phrase which might be applied to any well-to-do person, a banker, say, or a big shopkeeper. It was more than that.

'The son of a Pasha?'

They looked at each other.

'Could be,' said one doubtfully.

'More than that,' said another.

'More than *that*?'

The boy lost confidence.

'Not all Pashas are…like this, Effendi,' he said hesitantly.

Some Pashas were little more than crude farmers. This one was evidently not like that.

Owen had one last question.

'Has he been to the hammam before?'

There was doubt about the answer. The boys confessed.

'We think so, Effendi. But then he wasn't carrying a parcel and there was nothing to mark him.'

'Except his clothes,' one of the boys murmured.

'Has he been more than once?'

Again the boys looked at each other. Then two or three of them nodded.

Owen gave out some coins and then held up a handful more.

'These, too, will be yours,' he said, 'if you run to the Bab-el-Khalk when he comes again.'

◇◇◇

Zeid, meanwhile, had been nosing about the Palace. He had not been able to get inside but had watched the servants as they came and went and had identified the places they went to after leaving. He found that some of them liked to frequent a particular café, where they sat and smoked bubble-pipes to relax after the day's work. There was a mechanic among them who worked on the Palace cars. Most of them belonged to the Khedive but one or two belonged to particular princes. Not just the cars belonged to the princes; so did their mechanics, and Zeid soon learned that in the Palace ownership was guarded jealously.

A mechanic who worked for a prince worked for that prince and none other, and on his car and no others. Zeid learned, too, that this applied in other areas as well. Each prince was surrounded by his own retainers, who were blindly loyal to him alone. Among other things they guarded their prince's confidentiality and wouldn't answer questions about him or his doings.

To his surprise, Zeid found this was generally true of the Palace servants. Although they let slip the occasioned remark about what went on in the Palace, they were in general astonishingly reticent. Zeid worked out later that this reticence had something to do with the fierce-faced men he had previously run into at the Palace, the ones who so ostentatiously fingered the daggers at their belts.

Zeid realised that it was not going to be as easy to penetrate the Palace as it was to get into virtually any other institution in Cairo. He pondered this for some time and then came to Owen with a proposal.

Boys, he pointed out, could get in where grown men couldn't; and a boy like Salah, street-wise and besotted with motor cars, might well be acceptable where he himself wasn't.

They had a word with Salah, and the next day he presented himself at the Khedive's garages, having in some miraculous way by-passed the Palace's defences en route.

For a long time he hung around doing nothing, just gazing wide-eyed at the cars inside. Gradually he crept forward and put the occasional question. Since he was so knowledgeable, the men began to answer them. When they needed a particular tool, he knew exactly which one it was and put it in their hand almost before they recognised their need. Since he was so willing and so admiring he soon became part of the furniture.

He particularly admired the drivers. The drivers were exalted beings, even more exalted—in their opinions—than the mechanics. They, too, appreciated being appreciated and Salah took to sitting down beside them when they had their cup of tea. Gradually he became part of their circle, too.

Some time later, when the conversation was especially relaxed, he dared to confess his ambition: he wanted to become a driver, too.

They fell about laughing.

'Look, sonny,' they said, not unkindly, 'this is not an ordinary job. It's a big job. It requires skill.'

'I can see that,' said Salah.

'And judgment. And experience. It's not something that anyone can do. You've got to work up to it.'

'That's right!' said Salah. 'When I watch you, I see what had gone into it.'

'Maybe when you're a bit bigger,' they said kindly.

'There's obviously a lot to learn,' said Salah. 'I just wanted to make a start. Maybe as a first step I could become an assistant.'

'Well, we don't really have assistants.'

'Maybe you should. It's a big job, after all. And it's not right that men of your stature should be doing the polishing. I would polish until it shone.'

'Yes, but polishing is one thing, driving quite another.'

'Oh, I can see that.'

'First things first. Can you even drive?'

'I've got a pretty good idea,' said Salah.

'Yes, but what did you learn on. Not a car like these. Some of these cars here have got a lot of power under the bonnet. Do you know what speed that Brazier goes at?'

'Sixty,' said Salah.

'Yes, well, that's a lot to handle.'

'What about the De Dion?' asked Salah. 'Even more?'

'Well, you could argue about that. The point is, a big car like this could run away with you. You've got to be able to control it. And that requires—'

'Experience. Judgment,' said Salah. 'Maybe I could work up to it.'

'Not a chance. You could do something to it while you were working. Do you know how much these things cost?'

Of course Salah did.

'Well, then.'

'You've got to be rich to own a Brazier,' said Salah wistfully. 'Or a De Dion.'

'*Really* rich!'

'But you don't have to own it to drive it,' said Salah. 'Look at all of you!'

'Ah, well,' they said, laughing. 'There you are!'

They noticed he had his eye on the De Dion and one afternoon one of the drivers said:

'Come on, sonny. I've got to drive it round to the front of the Palace. You can sit beside me.'

Scarcely daring to breathe, Salah sat beside him.

When they got to the front of the Palace, the driver said: 'Right, son. Now you'd better hop out!'

'Thanks, Naguib!' breathed Salah.

When Naguib brought the car back to the garage, all dusty, Salah took the duster from him and polished the De Dion until he could see his face in it.

The next day Naguib took him with him again. The De Dion was in and out several times that day and each time, when it was required, Naguib took Salah, and each time, when it came back, Salah polished it until it gleamed.

The day after that Salah was in the garage wheeling a tyre when a man came in and went over to Naguib.

'I'm going to take her out this afternoon,' he said. 'See she's all right for petrol, will you?'

Salah was intercepted by one of the drivers as he moved towards him.

'Hey, sonny, what do you think you're doing?'

'I'm going to ask him if he'll take me on as an assistant driver.'

'No, no, no! Prince Hamid doesn't want to be bothered by the likes of *you.*'

◇◇◇

'Prince Hamid,' said Owen: 'what do you know about him?'

'He's the son of Farukh,' said Nikos. 'One of the Khedive's brothers. A junior son. One of several.'

'Have we come across him before?'

Nikos frowned.

'About two years ago I think there was something—'

He went to the filing cabinet. Nikos' files were the wonder of the world; or, at least, of the small part of the world that the Khedive's intelligence system encompassed.

'Yes. Actually, three years ago. He was one of a small group of students whom we picked up. They had formed a club we didn't like.'

'Why didn't we like it?'

'Ottoman sympathisers.'

Owen nodded. It would have been during the War. With the Turks just across the Suez Canal they had been looking out for possible internal sympathisers.

'What happened?'

'Nothing much. We took them in and held them for a little while and then released them.'

It was what they had been doing at the time. Cairo had abounded in political 'clubs' ever since he could remember. Many of them were student societies. Usually they just confined themselves to debate but occasionally they went further.

'What did they call themselves?'

'The Vengeance Society.'

That would have been why they had been picked up. There were so many societies that you couldn't bother about them all and you usually went for the ones whose titles indicated a possible propensity for violence.

'And did they satisfy their desire for vengeance?'

'Not from what I can see. But they liked to talk about it.'

That, of course, was why they had been released. He must have judged that despite the ominous title, the main product of the club had been hot air. Much fiery talk, little fiery action: that was how Cairo had been at that time. Students were always like that so you didn't take it too seriously.

All the same, it was uncommon for a prince to be involved in one of the clubs. Not, perhaps surprisingly, since, while the political clubs might favour revolution, the Khedive's family certainly didn't.

'It was reported to the Khedive, I presume?'

You usually did that when the Royal family turned out to be involved in something. They preferred things to be hushed up and had their own ways of disciplining.

'Yes. It was definitely reported. Wait a minute: there seems to have been some problem about it. Because I have a note here as a follow-up that the Khedive came back and said he wanted *us* to take action. But then maybe he had second thoughts, for there's another note saying he's decided to handle it himself after all.'

'Perhaps Hamid didn't like the way the Khedive started off and there was a bust-up?'

'Or perhaps the Khedive's brother intervened. Anyway, whatever they did, seemed to have worked, for we haven't heard of him since.'

'Until now,' said Owen.

◇◇◇

Owen was working on the security arrangements for the visit of the Commission. They might be in Egypt for as long as six months, thought Paul Trevelyan.

'Six months!'

'They'll need to hear submissions from interested parties.'

'Yes, but six months!'

'The longer, the better,' said Paul. 'Then everyone will get bored and be ready to listen to our compromise proposals. Which I've already drafted.'

'Couldn't you put them in a bit earlier?'

'Heavens, no! Before people are willing to even entertain the idea of compromise, they have to go down the other route first. That always takes a bit of time. About six months I would say. The other advantage is that everyone else gets bored too. With luck, the whole country will go off the boil.'

Owen had to admit there was some evidence of this. Fewer people were out on the streets, demonstrations were more half-hearted, there were not so many attacks on people and property. Cairo seemed to be reverting to its normal side, that is, one in which most of the incidents could be attributed to drunken soldiery.

The fact was, Owen had to concede, the Egyptians were really quite excited at the prospect of the Commission. The newspapers were full of people putting forward their positions. All the political parties were staking out their claims. Even—a masterstroke, this, for which Owen took some of the credit—subversive organisations such as the political clubs had been invited to put forward their ideas and were busy scribbling away. It seemed to be working.

For the moment. What would happen when the Commission announced the result of its deliberations was another matter. Owen, planning ahead, was beginning to drop hints of need for a suitably timed holiday, even that long-deferred honeymoon, which Zeinab, caught off-guard for once, welcomed enthusiastically.

Meanwhile, however, there was much to be resolved. Where should the members of the Commission stay, for example? The answer was obvious: the Savoy, which was the most luxurious hotel in Cairo. And where conduct its deliberations? Somewhere safe, clearly. The Barracks, suggested the Army. The High Commissioner didn't think that would send out quite the right signals. The Commissioner's Residency itself? But that, too, Owen suggested, might not give quite the message that was desired. The Palace? But that was only for Royal visitors. Was the King of England coming? No, alas: it appeared that he was more interested in going to Paris.

In the end it was decided that the best thing to do would be to hold the Commission's sessions in the same hotel as that in which its members were based. It would mean that they wouldn't have to walk outside in the heat. And make security simpler.

But—and this was what Owen was working on at the moment—who would be making it secure within? Where would the guards be coming from? The Army? Owen thought not. Keep them out of it at all costs. The Police? Over-stretched, as it was. The Mamur Zapt's own staff? All three of them? The Police it was going to have to be, and he would have to talk to Garvin.

Just at that moment he heard a door along the corridor open and close. It was McPhee. He stuck his head in the door.

'Owen, may I have a word?'

'Of course.'

'I would appreciate your advice. It's that boy. You know, the one who caused the trouble at the race-track. Garvin has asked me to handle it.'

Owen felt guilty. It was he who had passed the boy over to Garvin when they had got back to the Bab-el-Khalk, and now Garvin had passed him on to McPhee, feeling, no doubt, that he himself had more important things to do.

'I would have thought one of your usual talking-tos—'

Youths were always being taken to McPhee's office. Usually it was for stealing dates from a market-stall or something like that. An indignant stall-holder had caught them in the act and called the police. The police, being uncertain what to do, tended to pass them on to McPhee. Both stall-holder and police expected that the offender would receive at least a good thrashing. McPhee, however, a kindly man, didn't believe in thrashings. He believed that if they were taken to the Bab-el-Khalk and confronted with his own awful majesty, then that would be sufficient. Sometimes it was, too. The boys would emerge weeping—and then, Owen suspected go straight back to doing whatever they had been doing when they were arrested.

'I've given him one,' said McPhee.

'And didn't it work?'

'He was certainly contrite.'

'Well, then—'

'He says that his sheikh has spoken to him and he won't do it again.'

'I would have thought that was sufficient—'

'No, no, it's not that. It's his general attitude. So *intransigent!* I don't know what's come over the young nowadays.'

'Well—'

'I thought perhaps you might like to have a word with him.'

'I would, I would. But—'

His conscience gave a kick. He had passed the buck in the first place.

'All right,' he said wearily, 'I will.'

'Thank you, Owen. I greatly appreciate it. I know you're very pressed. I would have another go myself but I've just been called out. A nasty incident in a hammam.'

Owen put down his pencil.

'A hammam?' he said.

Chapter Seven

It was the one in Shafik Street which he had been to earlier.

'Do you mind if I come with you?'

'Not at all.'

'The boy can wait. I'll speak to him later.'

'Of course.'

Owen put on his tarboosh and they went out together.

'I have an interest in this particular hammam.'

He told McPhee about the package.

'A bomb!' said McPhee, aghast. 'But this is a very respectable hammam!'

McPhee knew his hammams. He often used them himself. Unmarried and living alone, and slightly eccentric anyway, he had embraced Egyptian culture enthusiastically, eating out in small native cafés most evenings, going to Egyptian theatre, which was not like going to English theatre, and in his spare time pursuing an almost antiquarian interest in traditional Egyptian ritual.

'You must take a look at the maghtas,' he told Owen now.

The maghtas were the small hot-water tanks one of which he had seen the lobster-like man emerge from.

'Why?'

'I think they're very old. Could be Roman. They remind me of the hot baths of Caracalla.'

'Caracalla?'

'In Rome. Where everyone used to bathe. Including the Emperors. One of them died there.'

'Really?'

'Yes. In the bath.'

It was just the sort of thing McPhee would know.

'Is that so?'

'Yes. They're made of stone, you see. Just like the Roman ones. And about the same dimensions.'

'Fascinating!'

'It is, isn't it?' said McPhee enthusiastically. 'I have a theory—'

Yes, McPhee would.

'—that the Egyptian hammam owes a great deal to the Roman system.'

'And this incident today?' Owen gently piloted McPhee back to the mundane present.

'Dreadful! A man murdered! While he was lying there.'

'In the tank? Boiled?'

McPhee looked at him reproachfully.

'Owen! How could you!'

'Sorry, sorry, sorry! I thought you said while he was lying there?'

'On a liwan, Owen, on a liwan. A couch. Not in the maghta.'

'I'm sorry. It's just that I was there today, and it seemed so hot—'

'He was strangled, Owen. I think. Although it's not entirely clear. But while he was massaged on a liwan, Owen. *Not* while he was in the maghta.'

'I'm sorry. Foolish of me. Strangled, you say?'

'Yes.'

'Accidentally?'

McPhee stared at him.

'Owen, what are you saying? He was *strangled.* How could that be accidental?'

'Well, you never know. While he was having his neck massaged, I mean, they're so vigorous …'

His voice died away.

'Owen, are you all right? It's been very hot lately.'

'No, no. It's just that I saw them at it. And it was so vigorous. They pull the head this way and that way—'

'He was *strangled*, Owen. That's a bit different.'

'Yes, yes. Of course.'

McPhee continued to look at him from time to time in a puzzled way.

◇◇◇

The hammam had a towel draped over the door.

McPhee, a respectable man, stopped.

The m'allim rushed out.

'It was all I could think of, Effendi. To stop people coming in. I thought you would not wish people to see—'

'No, no,' said McPhee. 'Quite right. And…there are no women in there?'

'Absolutely none, Effendi.'

There was a policeman, however, at the door, in the small reception area. He saluted when he saw them.

'Effendis!' he said with relief.

'He's been not letting anyone leave,' said the m'allim.

'Quite right!' said McPhee.

The m'allim plucked at his sleeve.

'They are getting angry, Effendi.'

A voice from inside said loudly:

'How much longer!'

McPhee went in. He was the person, in principle, who was in charge. The incident had been reported as an ordinary crime and the initial dealing with that report was the responsibility of the police and not the Mamur Zapt. What they had to do was confirm that there had been a crime and sort out any immediate aftermath. Then they would report it to the Parquet.

'I am sorry, gentlemen, that you should have been detained. You will understand, however, that in these dreadful circumstances—'

'I don't mind being detained for a bit,' said someone. 'But for two hours!'

It was Owen's acquaintance of the previous day.

'He's worried what his wife will say,' said someone else.

'She won't believe me,' said the fat man ruefully.

'We'll support you, Fehmi!' the other men chorused. 'Just refer her to us.'

'She won't believe you, either,' said the fat man sadly.

'How much longer do we have to wait here?' demanded one of the other men.

'Did any of you see anything?' asked McPhee.

'How could we? We were here, in the meslakh.'

'And the—the—?'

'In the harara, Effendi,' said the m'allim.

'So none of you actually witnessed—?'

'None of us, Effendi. And this oaf—'

He looked balefully at the constable, who felt compelled to defend himself.

'I thought I shouldn't let anyone go, Effendi. Not until you came.'

'Quite right. But now, I think, if you gentlemen are sure you can't help me... Just let me have your names, please. And where you live or can be contacted. Perhaps you could write them down?' he said to the constable.

'Well, um, Effendi...'

The constable could write but very slowly.

'Here,' said one of the bathers impatiently, 'let me do it. Abou? Suleiman?'

Owen went on into the first chamber, the beyt-owwal. It was empty, everyone having come through into the meslakh. He continued into the harara. Towelled, glum forms lay on the couches.

'Police,' said Owen. 'Where is he?'

They pointed across the room to where a still form lay on one of the slabs.

Owen went across to him. McPhee joined him.

'He's not been strangled,' said Owen. 'He's had his neck broken.'

He looked round the room.

'Did any of you see?'

'Effendi, no. We were just lying there being worked on—'

'And he was lying there being worked on—'

'When Darwish said: "Hey! What's wrong with him?"'

'I thought he'd had a heart attack,' said Darwish. 'I jumped up and ran across and thought, this is not a heart attack!'

'Darwish called to me,' said another of the men, 'and I took one look and called for the m'allim.'

'And I came running,' said the m'allim, 'and saw—'

'What did you see?'

'Him lying there. With the head and the neck—'

'Who had been working on him?'

'Yussef.'

'Where is Yussef?'

'Gone, Effendi. He is not here.'

'Has he left the hammam? Or is he still here?'

The m'allim hesitated.

'I have not seen him go. And if he had gone, I would have stopped him and said: "What do you think you're doing, Yussef? Have you joined the ranks of the Pashas or something, that you no longer need to work for a living?" But I did did not see him.'

'Is there a lawingi here?'

There were two of them, both in loin-cloths, both rather darker than the ordinary Egyptian, coming from the south, probably.

'Right, you come with me.'

He left McPhee to deal with the body and went through the hammam with the two lawingis, getting them to show him any hiding place that Yussef might be in. When they got to the back of the hammam he saw that it wasn't necessary, for there was a door at the back which was open.

'This man, Yussef,' he said. 'Did you see him?'

One of the lawingi seemed in a state of shock. He kept opening and closing his mouth, unable, it seemed, even to speak. The other lawingi seemed equally stunned, but he at least managed speech.

'He was at work, Effendi. As usual. Just the other side of the harara.'

'You did not see him do anything to the one he was working on? Anything different?'

'No, Effendi. No!'

The other lawingi at last managed to speak.

'No, Effendi!'

'And did you see him go? Leave the harara?'

'Effendi, I was working. When you are working, you do not see things.'

'What sort of man was he? This Yussef?'

'I did not know him well. He joined us only last week.'

Owen took them back into the harara. He led them across to the body.

'You are both lawingi. Men skilled in the arts of the hammam. How easy would it be for a lawingi to break a man's neck?'

The two men looked at each other.

'It would not be difficult, Effendi. When you are turning the head, you lift it a little. It would be easy to lift it a little more and give it an extra thrust.'

'But we wouldn't do that, Effendi,' broke in the other lawingi, finding his tongue. 'We know what we can do and what we should not. Each one of us has been taught, and our master would not let us go unless he was satisfied that we would not inadvertently do harm when we practised.'

'But you would know how,' said Owen, 'should you wish to do it not inadvertently?'

◇◇◇

The other bathers, who must have been in the harara for some time now, were being allowed to leave and had gone through into the meslakh to change. The harara was now empty, apart from the two lawingi and the body. The m'allim came back from the meslakh and stood near Owen wringing his hands.

'Effendi, what shall I do? Should I close the hammam?'

'You'll probably have to, at least for the day. The Parquet will be here soon and will tell you what they want.'

'But, Effendi, with *that* there...' He looked fearfully over to the side of the room where the body rested.

'It will not have to stay long,' Owen assured him. 'The Bimbashi will already have sent for the ambulance. But it must stay here until the Parquet have seen it.'

He sent the two lawingi off to their room. It was insufferably hot in the harara. He took off his jacket.

'Effendi, it cannot be allowed to stay here long. In the heat—'

'It will be gone long before it starts to smell,' said Owen.

He went over to the body. It had been covered with a towel. He pulled the towel off and studied it. It was the body of a man of about thirty, an Egyptian, and an Arab, not a Copt. The hair was neatly trimmed and the nails recently cut. He bent down and looked. Yes, the palms of the hands were slightly reddened from hilba. Hilba, after his previous visit, was still strongly in his mind.

He bent again and sniffed. Yes, there was a faint trace of the smell.

There were some contusions about the neck but the bruising was slight. That would not have been the case if the man had been strangled. Perhaps the post-mortem would yield more information.

He left the harara and went through into the meslakh, where McPhee was still taking names.

The m'allim followed him, still wringing his hands.

'Who will want to lie on a liwan where a dead man has rested?' he muttered. 'It was a beautiful hammam. The birds sang sweetly, the air was fragrant—'

'The birds will still sing sweetly, the air will still be fragrant,' Owen assured him.

'But men will say: here a man died!'

'In a few days, it will be forgotten.'

He asked the m'allim to open the locker where the dead man had left his clothes. In the closed space the smell of hilba was stronger.

And the smell of something else.

Owen had a very acute sense of smell, which was not always an advantage in Egypt. He stayed there for a moment, with his face pressed down to the locker. There were other smells there, of course, but yes, there it was again.

Had someone else been using the locker? That morning?

He took the clothes out and smelled them, and then put his head down to the locker again.

Whenever he did this he felt rather like a sniffer dog, but smells were often significant in Egypt. They were different from those you would encounter in England, or even in India, where he had been before he came to Egypt. And they hit you more. Go through a bazaar and you would be assailed by the smell of spices, of cardamom and mint and sandal-wood. Move in a crowd and there would be a great mixture of perfumes. Men put on perfume, and everyone, but everyone, oiled their bodies. The hot, rank smell of the camels hit you as they walked past. The roads themselves smelled of dry sand, or wet sand if the water-cart had recently sprayed, like a beach in England.

Egyptians were sensitive to smells. Europeans said they weren't, or how could they put up with the smell of donkey and camel dung in the streets? But Owen's theory was that it was because they were so sensitive to smells that they tried to disguise the smells around them with the sharper, more pungent perfumes that they put on.

Would there ever have been a discussion in England such on the one he'd heard in the hammam the day before? About the smells of different nationalities? Owen didn't know if he agreed with them, he would never previously thought in those terms, but he could allow the possibility.

He went back into the harara and smelled the body again. Yes, there it was, quite definite: the smell of hilba. But not the smell of attar-of-roses that had been on his clothes in the locker.

◇◇◇

The man had been wearing a galabeah, the long, cotton shirt-like gown that ordinary people in Cairo still wore. There was a shift to European clothes, to shirt and trousers, which was more marked among the young and among those who worked on European-style businesses, banks, country houses, some of the big cotton houses. But the ordinary shop-keeper and stall-holder, all wore galabeahs. The fellahin, the people who worked in the fields, wore galabeahs, usually blue ones.

That, and the hilba, and the open sandals that he wore, told Owen that the dead man was not an effendi, not an office worker or one of the more prosperous classes. But nor was he of the lowest class. The material of the galabeah was too good for that. Somewhere around the lower middle, Owen would put him.

◇◇◇

Owen took the m'allim by the sleeves and led him into the harara and over to the body. He pulled down the towel.

'Do you know him?'

'Never seen him in my life before,' said the m'allim promptly.

'He has not come to the hammam before?'

'Definitely not.'

'He came into the hammam in the ordinary way—?'

'That is so, yes.'

'And went through into the harara?'

'Yes.'

'And then what? What is your system? Did he call for Yussef, or did Yussef go to him?'

The m'allim hesitated.

'If Yussef was known to him, he might have called for him.'

'But he was not known to Yussef, was he? You said he had not been here before. And Yussef, too, was new. He had been here only a week.'

'That is true, yes.'

'*Did* he call for Yussef?'

'I do not think so, Effendi. How could he have called for him?'

'So Yussef went to him. How does it happen? Do the lawingis wait and offer themselves when there is a need?'

'I don't mind them waiting,' said the m'allim. 'It's the customers I don't want to see waiting. Of course, if the lawingis are all busy, they have to wait a little. But the lawingi are told that if they see someone waiting, they should not leave him unattended. They should break off and do *something* to him. In *my* hammam,' said the m'allim proudly, 'no one should wait. They should at least bring a cage over and let the bird sing to him.'

'So any of the lawingi might have gone to him?'

'That is so, yes.'

'But Yussef did.'

'That is so.'

'What I want to know is: did he single him out?'

'That I do not know, Effendi. But—why should he?'

'If he did not know him?'

'My explanation, Effendi,' said the m'allim confidently, 'is that he was *magnoum*. Crazy.'

'You think so?'

'Well, Effendi, he comes from the South. And all those people from the South are a bit…well, you know.'

'If you think that, then why did you employ him?'

'Well, Effendi, there are degrees of nuttiness. You might think a man a nut, but you might not think he's such a nut as to go and kill somebody!'

'Did you not ask about him before you took him on?'

'Of course I asked about him!' said the m'allim indignantly. 'What do you think I am? My hammam is a decent place and I don't want *anybody* to think they can work here. There are people—you won't believe this, Effendi!—who come here with evil motives. We don't want those. Well, just the odd one or two, you've got to cater for all tastes.'

'So you asked about him? Who did you ask?'

'Muhammed Ridwan, was it? Yes, I believe it was Muhammed Ridwan.'

'Who could speak for him?'

'Yes.'

'Where is Muhammed Ridwan to be found?'

'Where? Well, I don't know—'

'But you *did* know. If you asked him.'

'In the *suk*, I think, Effendi.'

'Where in the *suk*?'

'Ali's, I think. Yes, Ali's. Ali the barber.'

'There had better be an Ali-the-barber. And a Mohammed Ridwan!'

The m'allim looked unhappy.

'Effendi, I swear—'

◇◇◇

Owen went back to the lawingi. The m'allim tried to follow him but Owen sent him to wait for the arrival of the ambulance. And the arrival of the Parquet officer.

'How was it,' he said to the lawingi, 'that Yussef came to tend this man? Was it just that he was the next customer?'

'The m'allim usually assigns the person who is to work on him. But in this case we were all busy. So he just pointed to the liwan.'

'And Yussef went across to him?'

'I think he was already working on someone. For did I not hear him say to Abdul: "Abdul, you take over from me on this one, while I see to the other?"'

'So Yussef made the man his own?'

'It would seem so, Effendi.'

'Is that often done?'

'Usually it is the other way round. A man calls for a particular lawingi.'

'Was it so here? Did the man call for Yussef, or did Yussef pick the man?'

'I did not see, Effendi. It may be that the man spoke to Yussef first. But he would hardly have chosen Yussef to massage him, for Yussef was new here.'

'Perhaps they had met someone else?'

'I do not know, Effendi.'

'Yussef did not say so?'

'Yussef did not say much, Effendi. I do not think he would have stayed with us, Effendi, for he did not seem to like us. He did not join in. There are things we do together when we are free but he did none of them. Nor would he tell us about himself.'

'I was surprised the m'allim chose him,' said the other lawingi.

'Why?'

The lawingi hesitated.

'He was different from us, Effendi. He was—harder. You would not wish to quarrel with him. We—'

'—feared him,' said the other lawingi.

'Yes. Feared him. No one would want to cross him. For fear of what he might do. He was not the right person to work here, Effendi. He knew his job all right, I will say that for him. But I think he would have put people off.'

'Did he put…the man off? The man over there? Were there words?'

'I think we would have heard them,' said the other lawingi. 'It was just over there. Especially if it had been a quarrel.'

'And then suddenly it was done, and Yussef was gone?'

'I cannot believe it, Effendi. That a man should die. So near. In such a way. But so it was.'

◇◇◇

The man from the Parquet had arrived and was standing in the meslakh talking to McPhee. McPhee was giving him his list of names.

'And the dead man?'

'We have not yet established his identity,' said McPhee.

'No? Did not any of the people here—' he looked at the list—'know him?'

'It seems not.'

'That seems strange,' said the Parquet officer. 'People who go to a hammam usually chat. What else is there to do?'

'Just so, Effendi!' said the m'allim eagerly, who had been hovering on the edge of the conversation. 'And in my hammam there is beautiful talk.'

'They get to know each other. Form friends.'

'Just so!'

'Often it becomes quite a regular circle.'

'A band of brothers!' said the m'allim fervently.

'Oh, yes?' said the Parquet officer drily.

'In my hammam, yes, sir,' said the m'allim. 'They come one day and they hear the beautiful conversation and then they come again. People from all over Cairo. The hub of the universe, Effendi. That's what we are.'

'I must mend my ways,' said the Parquet officer. 'That fact had previously escaped my notice.'

'Oh, yes, sir. The high, the low, the rich, the poor, they all come to my hammam.'

'Including the man who was killed.'

'That I cannot explain, sir. He was unknown, a casual dropper-in from the streets. A stranger to us. Why, out of all the others, should he choose my hammam? To come to and be murdered?'

'That is hardly his fault.'

'It leaves a smear, sir. Who would want to lie on a liwan where a dead man has lain?'

'Do not tell them,' said the Parquet officer. 'Don't tell them which.'

'But people come and go,' said the m'allim, wringing his hands. 'They come here and they talk, and they will hear and then go and spread it all over Cairo!'

'Let me see the body,' said the parquet officer, cutting him short.

◇◇◇

Owen went outside. A dark, box-like carriage with no window had pulled up outside the hammam. It was the police ambulance come to take away the body.

The beggar boys were inspecting it with interest.

They clustered round Owen.

'Well, Effendi, tell us the latest!'

Owen laughed.

'I am sure you know already,' he said.

'A man was killed—'

'Yes. And do you know which man?'

'We think we have worked it out, Effendi.'

'I'll bet you have.'

'A man in a galabeah?'

'Yes. But there must be many such who come to the hammam.'

'We remember this one, Effendi, because when we saw him before he was talking with that man you asked us about, the one who did not see us but treated us as ants.'

'The one who carried the package in?'

'We think so, Effendi. But when we saw him the first time he wasn't carrying a package. The other man was waiting for him outside the hammam. They greeted each other and went in together, talking, and we thought this was strange, the one man so high that he did not even see us, and the other man, well, not low, but not one whom you would have thought the other one would have talked to. But they talked, and they came out together in a little while, talking. And then the high and mighty one went one way, and the man who is now dead went another.'

'Did the high and mighty one come in a car or in a carriage?'

'Car!' said the boys, amazed.

'He might have done,' said Owen.

'If he did, he must have left it. For when we saw him he was on foot.'

Owen distributed some more coins.

'When I saw you before, I promised that there would be more coins if you reported to me when the high and mighty one came again. I do not think he will be coming again. However, I give you the coins. And there could be more. Do you know the lawingi who work in the hammam?'

'Yes, Effendi.'

'Do you know the man, Yussef?'

'Is he the new one who came last week?'

'Yes. I do not think he will be coming again, either. But for anything you can find out about him, I will pay.'

◇◇◇

Two men came out of the hammam carrying a stretcher. On it lay a figure covered with a sheet. The men opened the rear of the ambulance and began to feed the body in.

One of the beggar boys plucked at Owen's sleeve.

'If we could see his face, Effendi, we could tell you if he was the man we thought.'

Owen hesitated.

Then he signed to the stretcher-bearers.

'Wait!'

He pulled the sheet down from the man's face.

'He is the one we thought,' said the boy.

◇◇◇

Owen went back into the hammam. The m'allim had opened the lockers and the Parquet officer was looking at the dead man's things. In the valuables locker was a red leather purse, a watch, and a ring.

The Parquet officer tipped up the purse and shook out some coins. There were some notes in it and he took those as well. He looked at the purse closely and then at the watch.

'No name,' he said. 'Still no name.'

Owen picked up the ring. It was a plain metal one, very worn, and with some faint scratches on the side. It looked rather like the ones used for ringing birds.

'A Pasha's ring,' said the Parquet man.

By which he meant not a ring owned by a Pasha but a ring showing that the person who wore it was owned by a Pasha. Or, maybe, had been owned by a Pasha.

Chapter Eight

Owen, mindful of his promise to McPhee, sent for the Helwan boy as soon as he got back to the Bab-el-Khalk.

He came in looking very nervous. He had probably never been in a building of this size before. The long corridors, the rows of doors, the large columns at the entrance, the huge flight of stairs, all had an effect when people were brought in. McPhee counted on this effect when he was addressing his homilies to the young boys. If it had an effect on the sophisticated young of Cairo, it would certainly have one on a boy from the country.

He stood before Owen, his eyes switching desperately from side to side, like a trapped rabbit.

'What is your name?'

'Yacoub,' he whispered.

'Yacoub, what you did at the race-track was foolish. It could have cost innocent people their lives.'

'I know. I am sorry. It will not happen again.'

'Good. Why did you do it?'

'I wanted to—to protest.'

'About what?'

'About what you are doing to us,' muttered the boy.

'What are we doing to you?'

The boy made a little hopeless gesture with his hands.

'Everything. You come from afar and bring us new things. But we don't want them. Why should we want them? They are nothing to us.'

'You are talking about the motor-cars?'

'Not just them. Everything.'

'The cars are new to me, too. They are new to everybody. But the world changes, Yacoub, and we have to accept that. And sometimes the change is good.'

The boy looked at him mutely.

'Take, for instance, motor-cars. You saw the men racing them, as men race horses. Well, that is not very important. But they can be used in other ways. Suppose there was someone in your village who was sick, and the hakim said: "We must take him to the hospital. And quickly, too." And all you had was a camel and a donkey. It would take hours and by the time you got him to hospital, he might have died. Whereas if you had a car you would get him there in time to save his life.'

'Cars are for the rich. They are not for the likes of us.'

'But they will be. That is what I mean when I say that the world changes. The thing is, one has to see that it changes for the good.'

'My sheikh says you have come here not to do good but to shake the tree. The fruit fall down and then you go off with them.'

'Perhaps first we see that the tree bears more fruit.'

'A tree bears the fruit that God decides.'

'You come from Helwan, don't you? And there it is mostly desert. But bring water to it and it will grow trees.'

'Egypt has known about water since long before the English came.'

'True. And great works were done in times past. But the English have brought new knowledge and that can only help more trees to grow.'

The boy said nothing. Owen wondered if it was worth persevering. But he wanted to try, though. He felt that this, if anywhere, was where the battle for the streets would be won. With the young. It was, he sometimes felt, it was not soldiers that Egypt needed but teachers. More Miss Skiffs!

Suddenly the boy said:

'You go off with the fruit but afterwards the tree is not as it was.'

'How is it different?'

'You have bent it into a different shape. That is what my sheikh says. And we can never go back to the old shape.'

'Nothing stays the same. Why should your tree be any different?'

'If the tree grows into a different shape, that is one thing, but if it is bent, that is another. And if it is bent by a stranger that is yet a third thing. Suppose you have a fig tree in your garden; and a stranger comes and bends it into a shape you do not want. Are you not right to resist it?'

'You may be. Provided you do it in a way that God approves.'

'Well, of course,' said the boy.

'But it is better to argue with the stranger and persuade him that what he seeks to do is wrong.'

'The English do not listen.'

'They do, if you talk long enough. In the City at the moment there is much talk among the great men, Egyptian as well as English. It may be that they will find a way forward. But if they do not, it is still a better way than striking blows.'

'Our sheikh says that it may be necessary to strike blows first and then have the arguments.'

There it was again. Back to the sheikh, always back to the sheikh. This was true, perhaps, less in the city than it was in the countryside, but the sheikhs, the religious ones, that was, had enormous power over the minds of people. And it started so young. The mind-set was formed so early, with its implications and its rigidities. It was no wonder that when they got to university or college they could so easily be brought out on the streets.

The other side of it was that listening to their sheikhs they developed an early capacity for dialectics. Arabs liked argument. In what was still a largely oral culture the capacity to argue was valued. That was why it was worth trying.

The trouble was that with the capacity for argument went all these rigidities!

But that was why McPhee had the youngsters in to see him rather than give them a thrashing. He hoped he could win them over. He seldom did but Owen respected him for trying. He tried to do it himself, usually with older students. And probably with a similar lack of success.

As was happening now. He wasn't getting anywhere. He'd better put a stop to it. He'd spent enough time on this boy. He wondered why McPhee had asked him to see him.

'The trouble with blows,' he said, 'is that they do not always fall on those who deserve them. So it was with your attempt to stop the cars. The innocent suffered.'

'I know,' said the boy, in a low voice. 'It was terrible.'

'Well, you see that now. And your sheikh has told you not to do it again.'

'I will not do it again. Although I do not like the cars.'

'Good.'

Owen went to stand up, to signal that the interview was at an end.

'But I will still strike a blow,' said the boy defiantly.

Owen sat down again.

'I thought that your sheikh had told you not to?'

'He told me not to go to the races again.'

'Well, then?'

'But to strike my blow in another way.'

Owen sighed. Perhaps this was why McPhee had sent the boy. He had thought the boy was going to cause trouble some time and that maybe he had better be put out of harm's way.

'What way?'

The boy's face lit up.

'He told me to go to the City. There I would find others who thought as I did. And we would band together and raise a great shout. And walk through the streets demanding justice and God's Law. And the walls of the City would come tumbling down. And the rotten tree would fall. And the stranger would be cast out of the gates. And the world would become clean.'

'Clean?'

'That is what my sheikh says.'

And now Owen could see why McPhee had sent the boy to him. From time to time they came across this kind of apocalyptic talk. And when they did they would always take it seriously. At the back of every English administrator's mind was what had happened not many years before in the Sudan, that vast country lying immediately to the south of Egypt and governed now, in Egypt's name, by the British. There had been similar talk there and it had been discounted as crazy rubbish. But it had spread and suddenly the Government had found itself with an enormous revolutionary movement on its hands and had had to fight a war before it could be put down.

Of course, the Sudan was not Egypt. Egypt was a much more developed country and far more sophisticated. It could never happen there.

But if it did, it might happen something like this. A crazy sheikh in a village, a boy spreading the word. McPhee was right to alert him.

There was something else, too.

'The sheikh told you that you would find others in the City who thought as you did?'

'That is so, yes.'

'How would you find them?'

But the boy realised he had said enough. He would say no more. Owen told him to forget about the people waiting in the City and go back to his village and stay there, or he would find himself in the caracol.

The boy went out, still defiant. Well, Owen didn't mind that. It didn't pay to beat the young down. But he would have to keep an eye on the situation. Starting with that sheikh in the village. He would ask the local mamur for a report.

But there was something closer to home. What was happening in the City? The boy had spoken as if there was some kind of movement there in the making. He would tell Nikos to get his men out and find out if there was. The last thing they wanted just at the moment was a religious insurrection as well. They had enough trouble on their hands already.

◇◇◇

Although Mahmoud and his wife were friends, Owen and Zeinab had not seen them for a while. This was important to Zeinab because since they had last met, Aisha's status had changed dramatically. She had become a mother.

Zeinab was quite interested in this. She knew, in theory, that this sort of thing was liable to happen. In practice, however, she had never had much to do with families and children. She had been brought up virtually alone in Nuri Pasha's vast mansion. There had been a brother, by another mother, but he was older than she was and she had never known him well. Just when there might have developed some comradeship between them he had fallen foul of the British Administration, and of the Khedive, and, indeed, of just about everybody else, and Nuri had been obliged to ship him abroad, where for the last few years, he had been happily gambling away in Cannes such allowance as Nuri made him.

Nuri, who had not known much parenthood himself, had tried to provide Zeinab with what companionship he could. He was actually a cultivated man but the cultivation he was steeped in was, as with most of the Egyptian ruling class, French not Egyptian, and Zeinab had grown up as a formidably intellectual French girl reading Proust with her father. This had not, however, equipped her to relate easily to other Egyptian girls of her age, nor for ordinary family life.

One result was, though, that she had grown up with a far greater degree of independence than most Egyptian women. Far greater, for example, than Miriam. She had been able, up to a point, to make her own life.

After a while she had chosen to make it with Owen and the seal had been put on their relationship when they had married. But now she had suddenly discovered that there were lots of things she hadn't picked up on the way. Sex was not one of them but family was. There were gaps, Zeinab decided, in her knowledge and it was time—she was, after all, now thirty—that she filled them.

She was, therefore, quite keen to see Aisha and ascertain at least what a baby looked like. When Owen mentioned his renewed contact with Mahmoud she decided that she would invite Mahmoud and Aisha round to dinner.

This was not quite as straightforward as it might seem. Egyptians never went out as husband-wife couples. Men went out with men. Women stayed at home. Mahmoud, however, considered himself a thoroughly modern man and believed this to be a practise of the past, one of many that needed reforming.

Aisha, as it turned out, also felt this, even more strongly than Mahmoud, so the invitation was promptly accepted and for the very next evening.

Here, though, there was another snag. Among the things that Zeinab hadn't picked up was exactly how you went about cooking a meal. In her father's house there had always been servants to do that. Owen, who like most bachelors, had usually eaten out at the Club or at the Officers Mess in the Barracks, was in no position to help her. Since they had married, and for quite a time before, they had always eaten out.

Zeinab, however, was no mushy new bride and knew exactly what to do. She commandeered her father's cook. The result was a very splendid dinner, the centre-piece of which was caille en sarcophage, although not one quite perhaps in the style that Mahmoud and Aisha were used to.

At some point in the evening the baby woke up and Aisha, with Zeinab in curious attendance, went off to feed it and change it. Seen naked, Zeinab thought, it looked very much like a puppy. Zeinab didn't care for puppies. However, for the sake of friendship, she was prepared to make allowances. Besides, puppies did not put out a hand and feel your face.

Owen and Mahmoud, meanwhile, were discussing politics. For Mahmoud the exiling of Zaghlul, the Wafd Party Leader, was a major mistake. It left a vacuum at the heart of legitimate politics into which all sorts of less legitimate groups might press. Owen rather agreed with him.

Aisha and Zeinab returned at this point.

'It may actually turn out an advantage to Zaghlul,' Aisha said. 'The British will realise they can't make a solution without him.'

Zeinab was surprised. She hadn't realised that Aisha was interested in politics.

'But has he the confidence of the Khedive?' she asked.

'Does that matter?'

Zeinab was quite shocked at this. For her, as for her father, 'politics' meant essentially the kind of intriguing that went on around the Khedive at court. This was the kind of politics she had grown up hearing about from her father and she had thought that was all the politics there was.

'But how can you do anything without the support of the Khedive?' she asked.

As soon as she had said it, she realised how naive she was. The fact was that even with the support of the Khedive, you couldn't do anything unless you also had the support of the British Administration.

'And the High Commissioner,' she added quickly.

'But he's not legitimate politics either,' said Mahmoud.

Legitimate? Zeinab hadn't thought much about legitimacy in politics before. For her politics was personal and all to do with the exercise of power. For almost the whole of her life she had been close to where power was exercised. She had heard her father talk of the latest manoeuvres at the Palace, she had heard Owen muttering about the latest foolishness of the British Government in London and what the Administration in Egypt might do about it. This was government in practice and legitimacy didn't come into it.

'Elections and all that sort of thing,' explained Aisha.

'There can be no legitimate Government without proper elections,' said Mahmoud.

Zeinab knew, of course, what elections were. She had often heard her father telling about how to fix them. But that didn't seem to be quite what was at issue here.

'It is surely what the Commission will be addressing,' said Mahmoud.

This new Commission! The one that was arriving the next day.

'It is so important!' said Aisha.

Was it? Zeinab had dismissed it as window dressing.

'Why?' she said.

Aisha stared at her.

'Zeinab, surely you know? It will give us our independence.'

It was what they all hoped, Owen knew. But—

'Perhaps not immediately,' he said swiftly.

'I don't think they can afford to delay,' said Mahmoud.

'Surely you want independence, Zeinab?' said Aisha.

'Well, yes, of course, but...'

Independence? she had always dismissed it as pie-in-the-sky. But here were Aisha and Mahmoud, two intelligent, informed people, talking as if it was imminent!

'But what, Zeinab?'

But what, exactly? Zeinab had a strongly practical turn of mind. She had always taken it for granted that things would go on much the same as they always had done. The British would rule, the politicians would deal, not much would change and she could get on with her life. But now here were Mahmoud and Aisha suggesting that in future things might be different!

Independence? An Egypt independent of the British, perhaps even of the Khedive? How *did* she feel? She hadn't really thought about it seriously before. If asked about it in a general way she would have replied, in a general way, that she was in favour of it. All Egyptians were. But in the same way as everyone was in favour of virtue, motherhood, and apple pie, as her husband sometimes said. (But what *was* apple pie?) But was she really in favour of it, on a down-to-earth basis?

What would it mean for her? How would it affect her and Owen? He would surely go along with what she felt. Wouldn't he? But *could* he?

She would have to think about this.

And meanwhile she would put the baby into the back of her mind.

◇◇◇

The Commission arrived and the High Commissioner held a Reception for them.

So much was obvious and so much was simple. But what followed afterwards would not be quite so simple.

The Reception was held on the Residency lawn, a beautiful spot for such an event, with fine English roses, beautiful Egyptian shrubs, and herbaceous borders to remind all decent expatriates of home. Turbaned suffragis in wide, scarlet kummberbunds brought round silver trays of small crustless sandwiches and other goodies, and in the late afternoon sunlight the champagne shone golden.

Owen, in his newly cleaned best suit, fresh from the front, circled among the guests. Paul was everywhere, introducing here, smoothing there, seeing that no one was omitted or neglected. The High Commissioner moved benignly from group to group, and the soldiers were all out of sight.

Except the Sirdar, the Commander of the Egyptian Army, or rather, of the British Army in Egypt, an important difference. He was in uniform and weighed down with medals and was talking to another figure with military bearing, only this one was not in the army but had come with the Commission, a man with military experience in India, which was, of course, seen as immediately transferable to Egypt.

He was saying something about the strategic significance of the Suez Canal.

'Absolutely!' barked the Sirdar.

'Vital to Britian's interest.'

'Damn right!'

'Oil.'

'Must never forget that.'

'Affects our position with respect to Egypt.'

'I should hope so,' said the Sirdar.

'What about all this unrest?'

'A little local difficulty.'

'You can handle it?'

'Of course!'

'The press is making too much of it. I expect. They always do. Hallo!'

'This is Owen. The Mamur Zapt.'

'Ma—?'

'Secret Service.'

'Oh.'

'The *Khedive*'s Secret Service,' said the Sirdar meaningfully.

'Oh.' Distinctly coolly.

'And ours, of course.'

'Oh, really? That's all right then.' Much warmer.

'Owen was in India,' said the Sirdar, who, despite his grave suspicions of Owen, felt he had to give the devil his due.

'Oh, really? Where?'

'On the Frontier,' said Owen. 'A while ago.'

'The Frontier, eh? Well…never was there myself. Always regretted that. Wanted to be where the real action was, but never quite managed it. Bound to a desk in Rawalpindi.'

'Someone's got to do it, sir,' said the Sirdar.

'That's what I told myself. I may be a desk wallah, I said, but deep down I am a soldier, and I want to be where the shooting is!'

Owen had heard that one before.

He moved away and ran into a large, rather four-square lady.

'Hello!' she said. 'I'm the token woman on the Commission. And the token woman here generally, by the look of it,' she said.

'Not so, Mrs. Oliphant,' said Paul Trevelyan, appearing beside them at that point. 'Over on the other side of the lawn I can see Mrs. Owen. I will take you across and introduce you to her.'

'An Army wife? I'm not sure that counts. Aren't there any Egyptian women here?'

'Mrs. Owen *is* an Egyptian.'

He led her across.

'Hello!' said Mrs. Oliphant. 'I'm the token woman. Are you a token woman too?'

'Yes,' said Zeinab.

'Now, come on, Zeinab, you're here because I love you,' said Paul. 'And there are many other women here, too, Mrs. Willoughby,—'

'So how do you find it, being married to an Englishman?'

'Dreadful!' said Zeinab. 'But I'm bringing him round.'

'Captain Owen isn't really in the army,' said Paul. 'He's in the service of the Khedive.'

'I thought you all were?'

'In a manner of speaking,' said Paul. 'Only Gareth is more genuinely in the services of the Khedive than the rest of us. He's the Mamur Zapt.'

'Responsible for keeping us alive?'

'You could say that. But other things, too.'

'I hope he doesn't allow his attention to wander!'

'Mrs. Owen works in a hospital,' said Paul. 'I thought you might be interested to meet her. Knowing your own work in hospitals.'

Mrs. Oliphant raised an eyebrow.

'You've certainly been doing your homework.'

'Your fame has reached even the Residency, Mrs. Oliphant.'

'What do you do?' asked Mrs. Oliphant, turning to Zeinab. 'Are you a doctor?'

'A manager.'

Mrs. Oliphant took her by the arm.

'Oh, really, my dear? That's most interesting. I should like to hear about it. I've just been having such a battle to get a woman appointed in one of my hospitals. A man's job, one idiot dared to say. Before I decapitated him. But that was in London. And now to come out here—'

'—to these benighted spots,' said Zeinab, who was beginning to rethink the advantages of independence.

'—and find that you're so much in advance of us—'

She led Zeinab off into a corner.

'Lovely roses, here, Willoughby,' someone was saying to the High Commissioner.

'They're my wife's pride and joy.'

'Beautiful fragrance!' sniffing them.

'We're very fortunate in Egypt. The climate is so good for growing. By the river, that is. You should see our sweetpeas!'

'I noticed the ones in the hotel. Lovely! The scent is everywhere.'

'Not everywhere,' said a short, squat man, who was perspiring vigorously. 'There was a damned great camel turd right at the entrance of the hotel. You'd have thought they would have cleared it away. And then there are all those donkeys just below the terrace—'

'Ah, the donkey-vous.'

'Donkey—?'

'Vous. Donkey-vous. It's where you go to get a donkey. "Vous voulez donkey, Monsieur?" That's what they say, and so it is called a donkey-vous.'

'Why don't they speak English?'

'They do, of course. As well.'

'I don't like it. Does that mean the French are getting in on the act?'

'Actually, they were in on the act before we got here. That's why so much French is spoken. Their legal system, for instance, is based on the Napoleonic Code.'

'You want to watch that. They could take advantage of that. You want to get them out.'

'In fact, we did get them out. That's why we're here.'

'Oh!'

A burly man was accosting Paul.

'What about the workers, then?'

'Working away happily,' said Paul.

'But are they working away? What's your unemployment figures?'

'They are difficult to ascertain in Egypt. So many people do casual jobs—'

'That's it! They need to get organised. What are you doing to help them get into unions?'

'Well—'

'Start with transport. Those camel drivers. I'll bet they're not in unions. You could start with them and then widen it out. First them and then the donkey-drivers. Not paid much, I'll bet. Get them into unions and then you'll be able to exert a bit of pressure. Drive wages up. Transport is a good place to start, you'd be able to get a strangle-hold.'

All over the lawn such conversations were going on. Owen felt depressed. Were these the people who were going to deliver Egypt's dream?

A man beside him was wiping the sweat from his face.

'Bloody hot, here, isn't it?'

'Warmish, yes.'

'They ought to bring fans out. Put them on the lawn. And not the old ones they've got inside. Do you know what? I looked at them and—can you imagine? In the Residency! The *British* Residency, they're all Swiss! What's the point of having a colony if you don't get them to buy British?'

'Actually, it's not a colony—'

'Or whatever. Amounts to the same thing. Money follows the flag, that's what I say. And the flag follows money!'

Meaning? Still, it sounded good. Whichever.

Behind him a loud voice was saying:

'Retrenchment and rigour! Financial rigour. That's what this country needs.'

Give them a country to play with and they were all happy. Like kids with a new toy. But, damn it, it wasn't a toy, it was a *country*!

'Aren't we going to be allowed out at *all?*' Someone else was complaining.

'Of course!' cried Paul. 'You can see as much of the country as you wish! Naturally we shall be working you hard, but I'm sure it will be possible to arrange a few excursions…'

'Not the bloody Pyramids again!'

'A mosque, perhaps? Or perhaps not,' he said hastily, seeing Owen, mindful of security, waving frantically at him.

'I was hoping to get to the races,' said a tall, thin man languidly.

'Races?' said Paul, taken aback for once.

'Perhaps the car races?' suggested Owen. 'Out at Helwan.'

Miles out in the desert, where there would be no security problems.

'That sounds promising,' said the languid gentleman. 'What have they got?'

'Braziers,' said Owen, 'and De Dions.'

'Really?'

'I was hoping to get out and meet the people,' said Mrs. Oliphant.

'And so you shall!' said Paul, beaming. 'Only you won't be going to them, they will be coming to you. To give evidence.'

'That wasn't quite what I meant,' said Mrs. Oliphant.

'We'll want to meet leading politicians,' said the man who had been talking with the High Commissioner about roses.

'Of course. Starting tomorrow with the Prime Minister, Rushdi Pasha.'

'We don't want just Government figures. We'll need to see someone from the Opposition.'

'Of course!'

'Zaghlul Pasha,' said someone.

'Well, now, that may be a bit difficult. He's actually in Malta at the moment—'

'On holiday?'

'Sort of.'

'Can't he be persuaded to come back to address us? He is the Leader of the Wafd, after all.'

Paul glanced at Willoughby.

'I'm sure that could be arranged. Couldn't it, sir?'

The High Commissioner swallowed.

'I suppose it could,' he said.

◇◇◇

When they had all gone, Owen said to Paul:

'They don't know anything about it.'

'That's right.'

'Except that bloke who mentioned the Wafd.'

'We'll have to watch him,' said Paul.

'It's the others I'm worried about.'

'Oh, I don't know,' said Paul. 'The less they know, the easier they are to handle.

Chapter Nine

Owen had decided that the High Commission's Reception was an important enough occasion for him to use his car and it was waiting for them when they came down the steps. As they were driving home he thought there were more people in the streets than usual and when they came to the Midan el Azhar he was sure of it.

'Do you mind if we make a bit of a detour, sir?' said the driver, 'looks pretty jammed ahead.'

'And perhaps I could drive,' said Zeinab.

'Not in these crowds!' said Owen.

'Maybe if I took you out a bit?' suggested the driver.

He turned off along the Sharia es Sanafiri and along the Bab-el Khalk, past Owen's office, as it happened, and then continued out to the Bab Zouweleh, one of the great gates of Cairo, where they turned north. Immediately they ran into columns of marching students, most of them in black gowns and carrying brass ink pots.

'Jesus!' said the driver, and braked hard.

'They're from the El Azhar,' said Owen. 'We'd better give them a miss.'

'Too right!' said the driver.

'Turn off down the Bardire,' said Owen.

They did, but then ran into more students, who looked at them with as much curiosity as hostility.

He had expected the latter. The students at the El Azhar, the greatest university in Egypt and possibly the greatest in the Muslim world, studied mainly theology. Some of them were carrying their books under their arm. Actually, not many of them had books. Instruction was mostly oral. You could see some professors in the crowds, dressed in their purple gowns. The El Azhar was seen, not always fairly, as a hot-bed of fanaticism. And the views of its students, on such subjects as cars and Westerners, might well be the same as Yacoub's. He had not, however, made sufficient allowance for the pull of the West, and a few of the students were inspecting the car knowledgeably and critically.

But not all of them. Some were looking at them fiercely and beginning to wave their arms.

'If you don't mind, sir,' said the driver. 'I think it would be best to get Mrs. Owen out of this.'

Zeinab had put on her veil again and Owen didn't think that would be enough. She was dressed in too many Western things.

The driver turned off down a side street.

He had just gone a little way along it when he had to come to a stop behind a bullock cart unloading heavy stones for a new building.

'Sod it!' said the driver.

There were not many students around at this point.

'There are some public gardens ahead,' said Owen, 'just down by the Bab el Ghoraib. By that rise. We'll get out and walk. Can you work your way round and pick us up by the Gardens?'

'Will you be all right, sir?'

'I think so. I'll take my jacket off and leave it with you.'

He had been in uniform for the Reception. Without his jacket, and in his shirt sleeves, and wearing the usual red Governmental tarboosh, he should be able to pass as an ordinary Egyptian Effendi out with his wife.

It wasn't far to the gardens but the streets here doubled back on themselves, taking them up towards the El Azhar. He could see its pinnacles and minarets rising above the houses in front of him.

Just at that moment a great column of students burst out of a gate and flooded along the road ahead of them. He pulled Zeinab quickly into a doorway.

The students, though, were not coming this way. They had turned right up the street and now were marching in quite an orderly fashion, chanting as they marched. It was part of a demonstration, of course. The students were always demonstrating, now more than ever. But what was it that they were chanting? Not 'Down with the Government!' Or 'Out with the British!' Something he was not familiar with.

'Say-ed Ali, Say-ed-Ah! Say-ed Ali, Say-ed Ali, Say-ed-Ah!'

Who was Sayed Ali? That was a new one. The ones he'd heard earlier, the big Wafd demonstration, had always been chanting 'Zaghlul.'

The last files of the column went past at the end of the street. Cautiously he continued up it.

The street at the end now was empty. There were occasional students but they were the law-abiding ones going in to their lectures.

Far away now to the left he could hear the chanting.

'Say-ed Ali, Say-ed Ali, Say-ed-Ah!'

He and Zeinab turned right down the street away from them and in the direction of the Gardens. It meant going past one of the entrances to the University but that was all right. There were other people passing too.

Through the entrance he could see the students clustered round the pillars. That was where they had their classes. The teacher would sit with his back to the pillar reading from a book or else reciting, and the students would sit on the ground writing down what he said on 'slates' of tin or yellow wood. Only a few of them would have paper, usually just loose leaves, and mostly they kept their ink-pots for writing after the lecture was over. They usually carried as well water-bottles and bread, which they put on the ground beside them, together with their slippers, which they took off when they entered, for the University was one great mosque.

No women were allowed, and Owen found it a bit incongruous to think of Zeinab, excluded, but reading Proust. Of course, you could look elsewhere: to the more modern university, over towards the Kasr-en-Nil, or the Schools of Law or Engineering, where, incidentally, a few women were allowed to study.

And yet, oddly, it was not, probably, from the traditional El Azhar that the bomb intended to be used against the Khedive had come. Behind that there was modern knowledge, acquaintance with science. And the knowledge of science was not yet so widespread in Egypt as to make you think it would exist far from one of the new university colleges.

◇◇◇

They walked on down to the Gardens, which had been flooded that morning. That was the way you watered gardens in Egypt: you flooded them with water from the Nile. A system of pipes led round to the main gardens and water was fed along them once a week. The water stood for only an hour or so but while it was there all kinds of birds came to delight in it: hoopoes and bulbuls and warblers and weavers, throwing the water over their backs, and buff-backed herons picking for frogs and beetles.

The car was waiting discreetly on the other side of the gardens.

'Better get those armoured plates back up,' said the driver dourly, as they drove away.

◇◇◇

Georgiades sauntered into Owen's office unusually early the next morning and dropped himself on the end of Owen's desk.

'Been talking,' he said.

'Oh, yes?'

'To the people on that water-cart's run.'

'You have?'

'Yes.'

'It's a regular run and people have got to know them. Hussein and Ahmet. They're getting to know me, too,' said Georgiades easily.

'Oh, good.'

'So they're more ready to talk.'

'And what do they have to say?'

'The drivers are part of the community. They do errands for people along the route. Pass messages. Deliver things.'

'Miss Skiff said those carts are like an unofficial postal service.'

'They are. And sometimes they deliver people, too.'

'People?'

'Old chap wants to see his daughter further along the route, gets a lift.'

'Well, that's very nice.'

'Children, too. A woman wants to deliver her son to her mother: puts the little fellow up on the box. The mother will be waiting for them. Very reliable, they are.'

'I suppose their route covers quite a lot of the city, too.'

'It does. But the funny thing is that they always call in at the hammam. There are other hammams on the route they take and they don't call in at them. But they do at this one.'

'I see.'

'They drop things in, pick things up. Regularly.'

'A sort of post office, is it?'

'Sort of. But the thing is, you see, that they're always doing it. They're very well known at the hammam. So if you have been getting the impression that what happened the other day was a one-off, you'd be mistaken.'

'Are you saying they might be delivering and carrying other things, too?'

Georgiades nodded.

'Drugs?'

The Greek hesitated.

'No reason to suppose that.'

'So?'

'Just thought you might be interested.'

'I am.'

Owen considered.

'I think it might be a good idea if you stuck around that hammam for a while. Go in and have a bath.'

Georgiades lifted himself off the end of the desk.

'Are you telling me something personal?' he demanded. 'Look, I walk around a bit. It's hot. It's true I sweat. But—'

'No, no. Strictly business, this is.'

'Right, then.'

Although after Georgiades had gone, Owen did wonder. What was it that Greeks were supposed to smell of? Camomile? Yoghurt?

◇◇◇

Owen went in to see Nikos.

'Sayed Ali,' he said. 'Do we have anything on him?'

'Which Sayed Ali?' said Nikos. 'There are dozens.'

'This is the one whose name they are chanting in their demonstrations.'

'There was a religious sheikh of that name,' said Nikos thoughtfully. He went to his files. 'But why are they chanting *his* name?'

'That's what I am wondering.'

'No, no, it's not that. Or not just that. He is a very popular, much venerated sheikh. The thing is, though, he's old.'

'That doesn't stop them from causing trouble.'

'Eventually it does. And now he's over ninety. Hardly ever leaves his house.'

'He could still be active.'

'There's not the impression I have. I gather he's rather frail. Doesn't deliver sermons these days. Doesn't see many people. Nearly blind, I think. Pretty much retired. From the world as well as religious affairs. That's why I'm surprised.'

'Has he any history?'

'Of political involvement?'

'Yes.'

'A long, long time ago. And not in Cairo, either. He moved to the City about twenty years ago. Before that he lived in the country. It happened there. And even then it didn't amount to much. Talk mostly. But inflammatory enough to attract our attention.'

'*Our?*'

'Your predecessor's. One of your predecessors. Predecessor but three.'

'That was a long time ago.'

'That's right. And that was the last time we had any trouble from him. That's another reason why I'm surprised that they should be chanting his name now.'

'Nothing more recent?'

'Nothing more recent.'

'And no sign of active political involvement?'

'No.'

'It sounds as if someone is wheeling him out. Using him.'

◇◇◇

Owen went over to the hotel where the Commission's members were staying. He wanted to check his security dispositions. He had men there in force. There were policemen, borrowed from Garvin, at all the entrances and policemen continuously patrolling round outside to see that no one got in at the windows. He had men on the roof. Roofs were significant things in Cairo. A lot of people lived there, for a start. Even more slept there, especially when it was hot. People were used to roofs. Thieves especially.

Most of the men were stationed inside. He didn't want them to be too obvious. Just enough to deter, not enough to antagonise the general population. At the front door there were just the usual burly policemen. But inside the door there were soldiers. He had been so short of men that in the end he had had to have them. And at the entrance to the corridor on which most of the Commission members were staying there were more soldiers.

Yet he wasn't placing most of his trust in them. What he worried about, especially following the attempt on the Khedive, was a bomb, placed in the basement or the kitchens or some other necessary but not obvious part of the building. He had Zeid continually checking such places. He hated using him in that way, it was a waste of a good man. But Zeid had a bit more security savvy than most of the others. He knew he could rely on him.

Georgiades meandered in from time to time, not assigned to anything special, but pottering around apparently aimlessly. Owen placed a lot of confidence in him. But he wasn't going to spend all his time there. Owen had other things for him to do: extending his acquaintance with the hammam, for example.

Nor was Owen going to spend much time there. However, he wanted to spend enough time there for it to be thought, especially by the members of the Commission, that he *was* spending pretty well all of his time there. That would reassure them and, according to Paul, reassurance was what they needed. And it might even, although he was skeptical about this, assist to deter anyone with evil intentions.

But he wasn't going to spend all his time at the hotel. For a start, he had too many things to do. And then he felt a deep-seated reluctance, which might even go back to his days on the North-West Frontier in India, to tie himself down to too static a position. Sure, have the defences up; but if you were in charge you should also be thinking more dynamically.

In any case, guarding the Commission was just part of the battle. He had to leave himself free to watch the other parts. And if he had set things up right at the hotel, that should be enough, shouldn't it?

The Army did not think so. They had an officer, a junior sub-altern, stationed in the hotel permanently, with a command point all of his very own. Not only that, the Sirdar came along personally to ensure that all was in order. He had wanted the soldiers outside. 'Manifesting their presence,' as he put it. Owen had insisted on their being inside. 'We don't want them drawing attention to the Commission's presence,' he said. 'That's inviting trouble,' but he could see the Army's point of view. That was the difference between him and the Army. The Sirdar was all for having things up front. Owen wanted to work behind the scenes.

He went round now to check his own dispositions and to think again whether there were any places that he had overlooked. He called in on the subaltern, who had seen Owen in the Officer's Mess on occasions, and therefore concluded that he was a sound chap.

'Not too sure about having the men inside, though,' he said.

'Better than having them set themselves up for target practice, isn't it?' said Owen.

'It bloody is!' said the experienced sergeant standing nearby. The young subaltern, not so green as not to know the cardinal rule of military leadership—'Follow your sergeant's advice!'—followed it.

◇◇◇

When he had done his rounds, Owen went out to the back of the hotel where his car was waiting for him. He had to get around a lot today and reckoned that he would manage that a great deal more speedily if he used the car and not an arabeah.

The car was waiting for Zeinab, too, who had been out to see her father that morning, and then done some shopping, and now needed to call in at the hospital to collect some papers.

As they were driving along they saw a familiar figure ahead of them and pulled to a halt.

'Can we give you a lift, Miss Skiff?'

'Well that *would* be very kind of you.'

'Have you walked far?'

'I have been out to the Nilometer to do some sketching.'

'Surely you have not walked all that way from the Nilometer?'

'Hillal was with me for the first part. But, really, I don't mind walking. You see so much more that way.'

'We are just calling in at the hospital. And then we can drop you right back to the Mission.'

'Well, that would be—'

When Miss Skiff had settled herself comfortably in the car, she said: 'I have not forgotten.'

'Forgotten?'

'About the water-cart. You asked me to find out whether any of my ladies had seen it that day before it got to the Sharia Nubar Pasha.'

'Oh, yes?'

'I wasn't sure whether I should enlist my colleagues at first. It might turn out to be the disadvantage of those two drivers and I would not wish it to do that. But then I thought that perhaps I shouldn't feel too sorry for them for if things had gone the way they intended, what would have happened to the horses? So, well, I did ask them.'

'And were they able to help?'

'They all knew the cart. Or, rather the horses that pulled it. And, you know, that is really rather surprising, for not all of them were patrolling the roads on that route. What I am saying, Captain Owen, is that it appeared that the cart does not normally stick to the route that it should. They had seen it all over the place. Well, I thought you would be interested in that.'

'I am, indeed.'

'But that particular day, the one we are interested in, someone had, in fact, seen it earlier. Do you know Maria? A nice Irish lady. Well, Maria always does that district on a Wednesday morning and she looks out for the cart because at that point the children come out from school and run along behind the cart dancing in its spray.

'That particular morning, however, the cart was late, so they missed it. Maria came upon it later further back along the route. It had stopped and the two drivers were looking underneath it and fiddling around. She thought, as I did in the Nubar Pasha, that perhaps it had broken down. But now I think that perhaps we were both wrong. I think they were looking to see if the bomb was all right. Or perhaps they were even readying it. They wouldn't want to have too much to do in the Nubar Pasha, would they, where everyone was looking at them. They would want to make it ready so that all they needed in the Nubar Pasha was a touch.'

◇◇◇

When they got to the hospital, Zeinab jumped out and ran up the front steps. As she came to the top she nearly collided with an Egyptian who was coming out. They both recoiled, apologising. And then from inside the door came a woman's voice, saying in surprise:

'Zeinab! I hadn't realised you were coming back!'

'I just want to pick up something,' said Zeinab.

'This is my brother, Asif. I took the chance while you were out of the office to get him to come round and advise me on the filing systems.'

'That is very kind of you, Asif.'

'It is nothing, nothing!' he said awkwardly.

He was plainly not used to addressing women, particularly a woman like Zeinab. He was put off by her dress, for a start. She was wearing a European dress, which while black and sober, exhibited her figure in a way he really wasn't used to and probably thought indecent. She wasn't wearing a veil, either, (Zeinab had taken it off to talk to Miss Skiff). Generally, her attire was not at all proper.

But what was most difficult to cope with was the way she carried herself. She had run up the steps in such an assured way, not shrinking back as she should have done, and then addressed him so boldly!

He didn't know where to look.

'Zeinab is my boss,' said Miriam.

She was another one who wasn't wearing her veil. It was all right when it had been just the two of them, brother and sister, talking together in her room, alone. But to come out without it, into a public place where everyone could see her—

He signalled to her preemptorily to put it on and get back inside.

She didn't seem to notice his signals.

Or was she ignoring them? Deliberately? He frowned. He would speak to her that evening.

'Miriam is a great asset,' said Zeinab smiling.

All the time he had been talking to her, he had kept his eyes fixed firmly on the ground. But, of course, when he was trying to signal to Miriam, he had raised them. Now, as Zeinab spoke, he unguardedly turned them to her face.

She was smiling at him!

He reeled back in confusion. This was bold, this was brazen, this was—well! Almost wanton!

He didn't know where to look, he couldn't think what to say.

Pulling himself together, he muttered something at random and then bolted down the steps.

◇◇◇

Where, of course, there was the car, and, with it, Owen and Miss Skiff.

'Asif!' cried Miss Skiff.

Asif stopped and turned.

'Miss Skiff!'

All his confusion fell from him. He came up to the car, his hands held out, his face beaming.

'Miss Skiff!'

He seized both her hands.

'Asif! How are you? It's been so long—'

'I should have come to see you. I've been so busy—'

'Of course! With all your responsibilities at the Palace! You've done so well!'

'No, no, not really—'

'But yes! Everyone says so. The heights you have reached!'

'If I have got anywhere, it's all due to you!'

'No, no. You were always the brightest boy in the class. I remember you so well.'

'And I remember you, Miss Skiff. I would have been nothing without you.'

'Oh, you would, Asif, you would. You were always so determined to succeed. Whatever you had undertaken, you would have done well at.'

'Yes, but without the knowledge you gave me, without the education, I would have been nothing.'

'Your father would have been so proud if he could see you now!'

'My father. Yes. He was always very ambitious on my behalf. The family had to make sacrifices. It cost such a lot to send me to Victoria College.'

'But, of course, it was worth it.'

'Oh, it was worth it. It gave me the start that he could never have had. There were times when he wondered…but you persuaded him, Miss Skiff.'

'Not really. Your results spoke for themselves.'

'But we didn't know. We were an ignorant family. We didn't know what they meant. If you had not spoken to him as you did—'

'I feel very well repaid.'

'Miss Skiff, I must come to see you. I *shall* come to see you. I have been so busy lately. Not just the Palace. Family responsibilities, you know.'

His eye traveled back up the steps, but Miriam had fled back inside.

'You always took your responsibilities seriously.'

'I have been neglecting them. Some of them.'

'I am sure you will soon put *that* right.'

◇◇◇

'Is the whole weight of the Parquet,' demanded the m'allim, when Mahmoud arrived, 'to fall on my poor hammam?'

When Mahmoud had come to dinner, Owen had told him about the developments at the hammam and Mahmoud had decided to go down to the hammam the next morning and take a look at things for himself. He knew the relevant Parquet officer, Sadiq Lutfi, a little and rang him up beforehand to ask if he would mind if Mahmoud dropped in.

'Come whenever you like, Mahmoud.' said Sadiq Lutfi cordially. 'It will be a pleasure to see you.'

Mahmoud had not wanted it to appear that he was trying to cut in on the case. His relations with junior members of the Parquet were good. His reputation within the Parquet generally, if not with his seniors, was high and juniors tended to look up to him.

Sadiq was standing outside the hammam when he arrived, talking to the beggar boys. He hurried over to Mahmoud and they embraced in the Arab fashion.

'So, Mahmoud, you have an interest? How can I help you?'

Mahmoud told him about Hussein and Ahmet.

'They, too?' said Sadiq.

'Too?'

'This hammam is like a railway station,' said Sadiq. 'Everyone comes here!'

'My hammam is a beautiful hammam,' butted in the m'allim, hovering about as usual.

'Yes, yes,' said Sadiq impatiently. 'The hub of the universe. I know.'

'It is like a jar of honey,' said the m'allim, 'and draws by its sweetness.'

'Yes, I'm sure.'

Sadiq led Mahmoud inside.

'Would you like to see round?' he asked.

'Talk me through the case,' said Mahmoud.

◇◇◇

'Well,' he said, after Sadiq had finished, 'I can see that the next time I go to a hammam I shall have to be on my guard.'

'What you have to be on guard against,' said Sadiq, 'is having an enemy who knows that you go there.'

'Yes,' said Mahmoud, 'that's the point, isn't it? Several conditions were necessary for this to happen. The dead man had to come here regularly. His attacker, Yussef, had to be planted in the hammam, so that he could take advantage of the opportunity when it arrived. And then he would have to be able to assert his claim to the massage, possibly against rival claims.'

'Well, that's what he did.'

'Did he?'

'Yes. Apparently.'

'And the part of the m'allim in all this?'

'He says he had no part.'

'But the lawingi says he normally does.'

'And he certainly brought Yussef in in the first place. Have you got anywhere with finding Yussef?'

'Not so far. But I think I will find him. He seems to have been good at his job. That is, he was a professional masseur. The world of masseurs is surprisingly small. You tend to go to a master to be trained and there are relatively few of them. We should be able to find out who Yussef's master was—there's a sort of guild of them—and from that—since people usually keep in touch with someone at home—find out where he is.'

Mahmoud nodded.

'Let us know when you do, will you? And what about the other man? The dead one. Have you been able to find out who he is?'

'Yes,' said Sadiq. 'I think so. Among the valuables he handed in to the m'allim was a ring. A Pasha's ring.'

He looked at Mahmoud.

'You know about Pasha's rings?'

'There would be an inscription,' said Mahmoud. 'The Pasha's mark.'

'There was one. We were able to identify the Pasha. He has a small estate up towards Damietta. I sent someone over there. He has talked to the overseer and thinks he has made a positive identification.'

Sadiq looked at his watch.

'He's bringing him up,' he said, 'and taking him to the mortuary. I'm just going over there. Would you like to come?'

Chapter Ten

After the heat of the streets, the mortuary was cool. There were shutters on all the windows and they were closed. The bodies were kept in a room below ground which was constantly refrigerated. There was a strong smell of antiseptic.

A doctor came forward and shook hands.

'Hello, Mr. Lutfi. I think your man will be here in a moment.' He looked at Mahmoud 'Mr. El Zaki? I believe we have met before.'

'Too frequently, I'm afraid,' said Mahmoud.

The doctor shrugged.

There were voices upstairs and then two men descended.

'Mr. Iffat? I am Sadiq Lutfi, and this is a colleague. Thank you for coming. It will not take long.'

They went into an even chillier room where there were two attendants. They looked at the doctor questioningly and then pulled out what looked like a long drawer. In it was a form covered by a sheet.

Sadiq took the overseer by the arm and led him forward.

One of the attendants pulled down the sheet.

Sadiq tightened his grip on the overseer's arm.

'Do you know this man?' he said.

The overseer looked at the face expressionlessly.

'Yes,' he said.

'Who is he?'

'Ziki,' he said. 'That's what we always used to call him.'

'Thank you.'

He signaled to the attendant, who pulled the sheet up again. The doctor led them upstairs to a rather pleasanter room overlooking the garden. He left them there and went out.

'I don't know what his mother will say,' said the overseer.

'Tell me about him,' said Sadiq.

'He worked on the estate until about five years ago.' He looked at Sadiq. 'It's a small estate,' he said, 'up near Damietta. It's not really big enough, that's the problem. It was bigger but the Pasha has had to sell more and more of his land. The best land, what we've got left, doesn't yield much. It's too far from the river, you see, and we had to let some of the canals go with the land. It's a battle, that's what it is. We don't make enough from the cotton to be able to afford improvements and the costs go up all the time. So we've had to let people go.'

'And Ziki was one of them?'

'One of the first. He worked in the office, you see, and we couldn't afford him. Not that he minded that much. He was always ambitious, was Ziki, and thought he could do better somewhere else. Well, he probably could.'

'But he kept his ring,' said Mahmoud.

'For old time's sake as much as anything, I expect. He was always true to the Pasha. Been with the family forever. But he knew he had to make the break. Things could only get worse. The young Pasha went at the same time.'

'The young Pasha?'

'The son. There was only one. He's the one who will inherit the estate. If he wants it. I don't think he will. It was always a bit backward for him. The only thing alive there is the dog,' he said to me. 'And it's not going to be here for long.'

Of course, he was a different man from his father. The old Pasha lived for the estate. But Rashid, that's the son, had other ideas. "Cairo is where the money is," he said. "I want to go there while I can still get some of it."'

'And did he?'

'Doing very well, it seems. He works for one of those big banks. "Do you mind working for foreigners?" I said, when he last came down. "I don't intend to do it for long," he said, looking at me in a sharp way. I don't know what's in his mind. Maybe he's counting on the old Pasha going. He's eighty-five, if he's a day, and cannot go on much longer. And when he does go, I reckon Rashid will sell the estate. And then maybe I'll have to do what Ziki did,' he said, 'get out and find something else.'

'Do you know what Ziki found?'

'I think he worked for a carrying business,' the overseer said.

'A carrying business?' said Mahmoud.

'So I gather. Up by the Citadel, somewhere, I think he said. He does a lot of work for the prison.'

'Carrying?'

'Yes. Things for the workshops. Materials. Food too, perhaps. Doing all right, too, he said.'

'Doing so well as to cause him enemies?' asked Sadiq.

'He didn't say anything like that!' said Mr. Iffat, taken aback.

'You see, what happened to him didn't happen by accident,' said Sadiq.

'No. No, I can see that.'

'I wondered if someone had had it in for him?'

'Must have done, I suppose. But he didn't tell us anything.' A shade of distaste crossed his face. 'And now the poor bastard is dead. Got a wife and kids, too. And a mother. I'm going to have to tell her.'

'You don't have to tell her everything,' said Sadiq.

'No. No, I suppose not.'

He looked relieved.

'I'll just tell her he's gone. Yes, that's what I'll do. That's enough, isn't it? Enough for any poor mother.'

◇◇◇

Mention of the carrying business and of the prison was enough to enable the Parquet to track the family down and that evening Sadiq went round to tell the man's wife. Mahmoud didn't go with him. He went over to the prison, however, and talked to the driver of Ziki's cart. There was only the driver. It was a very small business.

'It was built around the single contract,' Mahmoud told Owen later. 'The one with the prison. Apparently Rashid—that's the Pasha's son—had got it for him. The old ties had carried on even in the city. Rashid was able to push business his way occasionally. But it never amounted to much. The prison contract was the main thing. But Ziki was grateful for that. It made enough for his family to live on.'

'And through it he met other carriers?' said Owen. 'And that's how he got to know Hussein and Ahmet?'

'That's what his driver said. He didn't know how well he knew them. He thought maybe he knew them in the way he knew other carriers. They're quite a fraternity, the carriers of Cairo. They all knew each other. There were places where they would stop and drink tea, several of them together. They would help each other out if there were parcels to be delivered. You know, if one was going to a particular place and the other wasn't. Messages could be passed on, too.'

'Messages?'

'News, of course. Gossip. But also messages, not necessarily from carriers. Other people used them as a message service, too. If you wanted to get a message to the other side of the city, you might well use a carrier. And, of course, the ones who make the same journey regularly, like Hussein and Ahmet, or like Ziki, tend to be used more, because people know about them and can rely on them. The driver says that a lot of messages have been passing lately.'

'To do with what?'

'He doesn't know. Ziki kept the message side to himself. But he thinks they're to do with religion.'

'Religion?'

'That's why I thought you might like to come with me,' said Mahmoud.

◇◇◇

They were going to see the dead man's widow. She lived in one of the little, cramped streets beneath the Citadel. This was one of the oldest parts of Cairo and it had been one of the most beautiful. There were still beautiful bits, lovely, crumbling old houses with marvelous fretted woodwork, box-like windows protruding over the street until they nearly touched those on the other side, and, when you looked down from the height of the Citadel, dark little gardens filled with cypress and palm. And everywhere minarets: the tower-like ones of Ibn Tulun's mosque and the fantastic ones rising from the Bab-es-Zuweyla and from the El Azhar, and the green-tiled ones of the En-Nasir mosque.

But in between these large, fine buildings were hundreds of little houses, packed tight together, dilapidated, their plaster pock-marked with age. The streets were often so small that there wasn't room to drive a cart.

'Ziki kept his up on the Midan. The driver sleeps beneath it. That is, actually, where he reckons he lives. Ziki used to come up each day and tell him where he had to go.'

They found the house and Ziki's widow came to the door, carrying a baby and with a small child clinging to her skirts. Inside, there were more children.

'How many?' said Owen, smiling.

'God has blessed us with five,' said the woman.

'That is, indeed, a blessing, although when they are small, it may not seem so.'

'It is a blessing,' the woman agreed. 'And will be something to remember Ziki by.'

'It will not be easy,' said Mahmoud, 'to feed so many mouths when there is no longer a man in the family.'

'Abu will keep driving the cart,' she said. 'As long as I tell him where to drive it. He is a good man but—' she tapped her head '—not one of the brightest. He will have to be told. But I can tell him as well as Ziki.'

'You know enough to be able to tell him?'

The woman nodded her head definitely.

'I know Ziki's work,' she said. 'We built the business up together.'

'What sort of man was Ziki?'

'An ordinary man. Too ordinary to be killed,' she said bitterly.

'And yet he was killed. Why was that, do you think?'

She shrugged.

'What does a woman know of her husband in the end? She knows him in the house, she knows him with his children, and she knows him in bed. And sometimes in his work. But who does he mix with when he goes out to the café in the evening? To smoke his pipe and chat?'

'He goes out in the evening, does he?'

'Most evenings. I don't begrudge him that. He has worked hard all day. He gives me the money I need for the housekeeping. He doesn't knock the children around. He doesn't knock me around. He doesn't drink, and that is a blessing, and an uncommon one around here. He was a good man.'

'You think, perhaps, he made enemies at the café?'

'Or in his work. What else am I to think?'

'You know his work. Is that likely?'

'No. Nor at the café either. But what else is there?'

'These are troubled times,' said Mahmoud. 'Could he have got mixed up in the troubles?'

'How?'

'Well, did he not carry messages?'

'He has always carried messages. Everyone does.'

'And he knew others who carried things. Did he ever mention the names of Hussein and Ahmet to you?'

'Oh, yes. He used to meet them at the café. They played dominoes together. But I have not heard yet that playing dominoes is a dangerous thing.'

Owen laughed.

'Nor me, either,' he said. 'But carrying messages could be a dangerous thing.'

'Carrying a message to say that a boy has arrived from the country? Or that Fatima needs some more cooking oil? Or that a child is sick?'

'Not all his messages were like that. I have heard that some were religious.'

'Religious? Well, he might have carried a message from our sheikh to Sheikh Abbas to ask him to do a funeral for him, but—'

'Did Ziki take an interest in such things? Was he himself religiously inclined?'

'Ziki? No man less. I have spoken to him about it. "You know where you will finish up," I said to him, "if you never go to the mosque." "God cares for everybody," he used to say. "Yes, but he's not even going to recognise you," I said.'

'Did he ever speak of Sayed Ali?' asked Owen.

'Sayed Ali? Well, there's a good man. If they were all like him! They don't make his sort nowadays. Speak of him? Well, everyone spoke of him. Even my husband, who, you would have thought, wouldn't even have known his name. But, yes, he had spoken of him once or twice lately.'

'What did he say about him?'

'Well, you know, everyone is saying that the dear man is going to stand up. And come forward and denounce the evil ways of the time. "Stand up?" I said. "The dear man has been bed-ridden for years! He *can't* stand up." Ziki got annoyed with me. "Be quiet, woman!" he said. "What do you know about it? He is going to say that the British must go." "British must go?" I said. "And what will happen to us then? What will become of your work? What we do for the prison gives us nine tenths of our money!" "There will still be prisons," he said, "even when the British go." "Well, the next time you see Sayed Ali," I said, "—and that won't be soon, if you carry on the way you're doing, not going to the mosque and such—you can ask him what will happen to the prisons if the British go? We'll all be out of work."'

'If he knew such things,' said Owen, 'might it not be that he carried messages to or from Sayed Ali?'

'About what? Ramadan, or something? Look, the Sheikh doesn't need advice from the likes of my husband—'

'To say, perhaps, that he was going to speak out, and to gather themselves in readiness?'

The woman stopped her flow.

'Well, that is possible,' she admitted.

'But you don't know that it was so?'

'No.'

As they were leaving, Mahmoud turned back.

'Didn't I hear that your husband has taken to going to the hammam?'

'And a very good thing, too,' said the woman. '"Not before time!" I said to him. "And if you were as pure inside as you were outside—"'

'"Oh, shut up, woman!" he said.'

◇◇◇

In the café men were sitting smoking bubble pipes and playing dominoes. They didn't seem to be doing anything else, apart from chatting. How the patron made a living Owen could not see, but, then, he never could. Egyptians did not go to cafés to consume things. They even brought their own pipes with them. Perhaps the landlord supplied charcoal but he supplied little else. The men didn't seem to buy beer, they went to lower establishments for that. There was some desultory drinking of tea and coffee but for the most part the clients just sat. It was a café used almost exclusively by working men, tired after their day's work and sapped of energy.

They looked a little curiously at Mahmoud and Owen as they came in but then went back to their pipes. After a while the patron came out from behind the counter and poured Owen and Mahmoud their coffee from a copper vessel with a long spout. They sat sipping it and watching a game of dominoes at the next table.

The game finished and while the players were setting up the dominoes for the next game one of them stood up and wandered over to where another group was playing.

'I wondered where those dominoes had got to,' he said. 'You must have got hold of them already when we came. I'd rather play with these than the ones we've got.'

'These are your favourites, are they, Riki?' said one of the players. 'I'll remember that; and look at them carefully when I'm playing with you!'

They all laughed.

As he was going back to his own table his knee accidentally caught Owen and Mahmoud's table spilling some coffee. He apologised at once and went to the counter for a rag, came back, and mopped it up himself.

'Sorry about that!' he said.

'It's nothing,' murmured Mahmoud, waving a depreciating hand.

The man took the rag back to the counter.

'Not seen you here before,' he said, as he came back.

'Just been calling in on Ziki's widow,' said Mahmoud.

'Bad business that. Who would want to do a thing like that?'

'I can't understand it, either,' said Mahmoud. 'Ziki wasn't the kind of man who would get involved in trouble.'

There were grunts of agreement from the men round the tables.

'Although you never know who you might come up against in that sort of business.'

He was watching the men carefully but no one responded.

'I don't know how his wife will manage,' he said.

'Oh, she'll manage, all right,' said one of the men. 'She knows as much about the day-to-day running of the business as he did. Probably more, since he's taken lately to getting himself involved in other things.'

'Ah, that's it!' said Mahmoud. 'I've been wondering. He's seemed a bit different lately. Probably got too much on his plate. What's he up to, then?'

'It's this Sayed Ali business.'

'Oh, that!' said Mahmoud, as if it explained everything. 'But, you know, that surprises me. I wouldn't have thought he was the man to get himself involved in that.'

'No. I know what you mean.'

'One mustn't say these things, not with him so recently—. But I wouldn't have thought he was much of a religious man at heart.'

'Oh, he wasn't!'

'But, anyway, I don't know how much of a religious thing it is,' said someone else.

'No? But Sayed Ali—'

'Oh, he's religious all right. But he's a hundred if he's a day. Doesn't get off his bed these days. Someone else is doing all the work.'

'Well, I hope they are. If only to spare him. You don't want care at his time of life,' said Mahmoud.

'No you don't.'

'Why's he doing it, then?'

'*Is* he doing it?' asked someone who had not previously spoken.

'What do you mean, Ibrahim?'

'Well, my wife's friend's cousin goes to help in his house and she says that these days he doesn't know much about what's going on around him.'

'His thoughts are all on Eternity, I suppose.'

'Well, so they should be.'

'Yes, but, wait a minute,' said Mahmoud, 'didn't you say how busy Ziki has been, with all the things he's been doing for him?'

'Ah, but that's not for the dear man himself.'

'No?'

'No. There are some people around him.'

'There usually are,' said Mahmoud. 'When you start getting old. And usually it's not religion they're interested in. It's money. Not in his case, of course,' he said hastily.

'No. These men have already got plenty of that. So my wife's friend's cousin says. You don't buy clothes like that at the

tailor's in the souk, she says. And there's one that comes smelling of—'

'Yes?' said Owen.

'Milk and honey and—'

'Oh!'

'Roses. That's what she says. Smells like a Pasha's garden.
That's what she says.'

◇◇◇

Nikos, as far as Owen knew, had no existence outside the office.
He was always there before anyone else in the morning and
stayed on alone after everyone had gone in the evening. Owen
suspected that when the day was done he climbed into one of
his filing cabinets and stayed there until the next morning.

All Egyptian life was in his filing cabinets. His records were
immense, comprehensive and exhaustive; and only Nikos had
access to them. This, of course, made him indispensable, and
the Copts had learned over the centuries, under a succession of
nominal rulers, how to make sure that they could not be done
without. It was, thought Owen, the bureaucratic instinct, dis-
tilled to a quintessence.

But it was also very useful.

Nikos came in the next morning with a smile of satisfaction, rare
for him—he didn't believe in giving secrets away—and put two large
files on Owen's desk. Owen looked at him questioningly.

'They are?'

'The Hamid circle.'

'Prince Hamid? The De Dion owner?'

'And owner of much else besides.'

Owen looked at the bulky files.

'Give me the essence,' he said.

'A man, as I think I said to you, of enthusiasms. His first
enthusiasm was for night clubs and all that went with them:
drink, drugs, gambling, and women. And, of course, ultimately
venereal disease. This rather shocked him as he had thought that
as a member of the royal family he was immune to such things. His

father put him right. The disease was, in fact, unusually intractable and he spent a prolonged time in a French hospital.

'From this he emerged a more sober man, but still one given to enthusiasms. His next enthusiasm was for learning and he wanted to go to a university, preferably a French one. His father, however, in view of his previous history, was not having that. Cairo it was to be, where his father would keep an eye on him.

'But what was he to study? El Azhar was clearly not the place for him. He had never shown the slightest interest in religion and the Khedive, who had a say in the education of royal princes, was totally opposed to it on the grounds that it was a dangerous thing for princes to meddle with. I tell you this because later Hamid appeared to have changed his mind.

'What, then, was he to study? The only thing that appeared to interest him was driving cars, so it was agreed that he should go to the College of Engineering. Actually, it was only the driving that interested him and at the end of his first year he had to drop out.

'By then, though, he had made some student friends. They were, of course, radical like all students at the time. You may wonder what a member of the Khedive's family was doing with radical friends. I think it was because he was a bit against his father, and the Khedive, and authority in general at the time and they played on this. Might he not, with his name, his influence and his talents have a significant part to play in the revolution that they were sure was going to come? Even—dare they whisper it—as leader?

'Well, this quite struck his fancy and for a while he dabbled in student politics. It was a time when they were all joining secret, revolutionary societies, and he was persuaded to join one, as I told you. He became, in fact, its leader. Nominally I suspect.

'They talked themselves into action. The action was to take the form of bombs. They talked of one of the bridges, perhaps the Kasr-en-Nil. They wanted to disrupt the war effort. They were all pro-Ottoman, of course. In the end it didn't come to anything because they talked too much and one of our people heard them. They were pulled in and Hamid was reported to the Khedive. He was given a good ticking off, which he didn't take kindly, and at one point, as I think I told you, the Khedive considered handing him back to us. And then it was all smoothed over, his enthusiasm for politics apparently faded, and he took to racing cars.

'Now I come to the interesting bit. The names of the people in the radical society he was a member of. There was no one else from the royal family. Student societies were a bit beneath them. But there was a Pasha's son. He was, I think, the real leader, although that didn't come out till later. At the time he was pulled in he made a great to-do about being a serious student of business, led astray by older friends, and anxious only, now that he had learned his lesson, to get back to banking.'

'Banking?' said Owen.

'His name was Rashid.'

'The one from the estate Ziki worked on?'

'That's right. They came up to Cairo at the same time and for a while they stayed together. Ziki was never a member of the society, he was too lowly for that. But he did things for the group.'

'"Did things?"'

'Obtained materials, for instance. For the bombs. He knew how to get hold of such things, from his experience on the estate. There was a quarry nearby. He was the one who was sent to prison. The students got off with a warning. No wish to spoil promising careers, etc. In fact, Rashid didn't forget about him. With Hamid's help, they got him out of prison after only a few months, and then Rashid found a job for him.'

'A carrying business,' said Owen.

'That's right. The money came from Hamid.'

Owen tapped the file.

'Where did you get that from? Is it in here?'

'The agent who had previously informed on them knew about Ziki. He was the one who had found out about the explosives. He came across him afterwards.'

Owen nodded.

'Then everything went quiet,' said Nikos, 'and after a while we reckoned they had moved on to other things.'

That was what usually happened with students. Like Hamid, they were creatures of enthusiasms, and when the enthusiasm faded there were back to getting on with their lives. That was the good thing about students. They usually grew out of it.

So what you had to do, what he had always tried to do, was let them grow.

It usually worked.

'And, until recently,' Owen said, 'we thought that they had?'

'That's what it looked like.'

Owen sat and thought.

'What evidence have we got that they haven't?'

'The De Dion and Ziki.'

'What's Rashid doing now?'

Nikos hesitated.

'That, perhaps, is also significant. I said that Hamid might have changed his mind about religion. Or be changing it. He has been to see Sayed Ali.'

'The religious leader?'

'Rashid took him. And Rashid himself seems to be spending all his time with Sayed Ali. Of course,' said Nikos, 'Hamid's visits to Sayed Ali, and Rashid's spending a lot of time there, may be nothing to do with religion at all.'

He went back to his office, leaving the files on Owen's desk.

Owen began to read.

After a while he stopped and went back and began to go through the names again.

◇◇◇

The Commission had got down to hearing people who wished to give evidence to it.

'Four so far,' said Paul, rubbing his hands. 'Only 179 still to go.'

'Bit slow, isn't it?' said Owen.

'The Commission wants to deny no one the right to make representations.'

'It will take years at this rate.'

'Why, so it might!' said Paul.

The Commission's members, however, were already beginning to show signs of mutiny. The hotel was holding a reception, another one, for its distinguished visitors. Prudently, they were holding it inside; less prudently, some of the members had strayed out on to the terrace in front of the hotel. Paul rushed out to coax them back.

'Look,' said one of them belligerently, 'I've been sitting in a room all day for five days listening to people speak Arabic. I don't speak Arabic.'

'You have transcripts,' said Paul.

'They are all in Commission-speak. I don't speak Commission-speak.'

'Nor does anyone else,' muttered the man beside him.

'I want to get out,' said the first man.

'Into the fields!' cried Paul. 'We'll go to see the cotton fields tomorrow. Cotton is very important to Egypt. It's the main industry.'

'It shouldn't be,' said the businessman. 'A big mistake, relying on one product.'

'I'm not sure you should jump to conclusions until you've had an opportunity to meet the representatives of the Cotton Board.'

'I don't want to hear any more representations. I want to get outside.'

'Into the fields! That's just what I'm suggesting. To see the cotton growing.'

'Is there anything interesting about cotton growing?' someone asked.

'Oh, a lot!' Paul answered him.

'What does it...do?'

'Do? Well, it...sort of...grows.'

'Like weeds?' said someone helpfully.

'Yes. No. No, not like weeds.'

'Likes roses, perhaps?' suggested the rose fancier.

'Yes. You could say that. Almost.'

'Wouldn't it be all white, though? I mean, the flowers?'

'That doesn't sound very interesting,' said someone doubtfully.

'And green,' put in Paul hastily. 'Green, too.'

Paul was not much of an agriculturist.

'I quite like it *here*,' said the man who had been interested in racing. 'On the terrace. With a drink.'

'I just want to get out.'

'I'll arrange something for tomorrow. An excursion, perhaps.'

'No thanks!' they said unitedly.

'Right,' said Paul. 'I'll see what I can do.'

From the far end of the street came the sound of confused shouting. It settled down into rhythmic chants.

'Perhaps we should go inside,' said Paul.

'Why?'

'More drink.'

'Oh, right, then,' said the racing one, and set off obediently.

Someone nudged Owen in the ribs.

'Playing hookey, are you?'

He turned.

'Don't blame you,' said Mrs. Oliphant. 'I've had enough of it myself inside.' She wandered over to the edge of the terrace. 'What's this, then? It sounds like a procession.'

'A demonstration,' said Owen.

'Really?'

'Perhaps we should follow Mr. Trevelyan's advice and go inside.'

'Not me!' said Mrs. Oliphant.

'Nor me,' said the Trade Unionist. 'I want to see our lads.'

'I don't think they'll be your lads,' said Owen.

'It sounds religious to me,' said Mrs. Oliphant, peering.

'It's political,' said Owen.

The head of the demonstration came round the corner. Something about it was puzzling.

He could hear the chanting more clearly now. It was not what he had expected. He had thought it would be 'Sayed Ali, Sayed-Ali!;' as before. But it was not. The people in the front were carrying a large green banner: and they were chanting 'Za-ghlul! Za-ghlul!'

Chapter Eleven

Paul came out onto the terrace and stood beside Owen watching the procession go past.

'I got the Old Man to let him come back,' he said.

'Zaghlul?'

Paul nodded.

'The Commission expressed a wish to see him. It's a perfect excuse. The Old Man can climb down without losing face.'

'His supporters are out already.'

'So much the better. That will persuade the Commission he's someone to be reckoned with. Then they'll let us start dealing with him.'

◇◇◇

'Can't have this!' said the Sirdar.

'Can't have what?'

'Everyone coming out onto the streets like this. It looks bad. Gives the wrong impression.'

'What would be the right impression?'

'That we've got everything under control. I'm sorry, Owen, it won't do. I've been talking to some of the members. Know one of them—that chap I was talking to the other day. Soldier himself. Understands these things. "What you need do," he said, "is crack down on them. Hit them hard enough and you'll only have to hit them once."'

'There are a lot of people you'll have to crack down upon.'

'I've got a lot of people to crack down on them with. It's different for you, Owen. I appreciate that. All you've got is half a man and a dog. Can't do much with that. I'm not blaming you. But the time has come to get a grip on things.'

Owen would have put it down as Army talk and forgotten about it; later, inside, he saw Willoughby talking earnestly to the Sirdar's military friend. Later still, the High Commissioner came across to him.

'I think we're going to have to try something new, Gareth. We can't go on like this.'

'We are trying something new. Now that you've let Zaghlul come back.'

'That's window-dressing. I've let Paul persuade me, especially since the Commission asked to see him. But it doesn't alter the underlying realities. It's not talk we need now but action.'

'And by that you mean military action?'

'Well—'

'It would be a big mistake, sir. It would set the whole country against us.'

'I knew you would say that. And you're quite right to. But I have to make a decision, and my decision is to tilt things away from the political and towards the military for a bit.'

'What exactly are you saying?'

'I'm giving the Sirdar a bigger hand. And I want you to concentrate on looking after the Commission. Oh, and the Khedive. We mustn't forget him. Have you got anywhere on him yet?'

'I'm getting there.'

'It's too much for you, Owen. You've got too much on your plate. It was my fault not to recognise that. Your turn will come again later. After the Army has put the situation to rights.'

◇◇◇

'I'm going to resign,' said Owen.

'No, you're not,' said Paul. 'Not and leave me to take on the Army all by myself.'

'It's a waste of time.'

'No, it's not. You know it's not and I know it's not. The political is the only way. In the end.'

'Yes, but there's a difference between your political and my political. Your political is the only way, yes. In the end the solution has to be political and at the Governmental level. But at my level it's really just a question of stopping things from coming to a head.'

'But what's wrong with that?' cried Paul.

'Maybe it would be better if we *let* things come to a head.'

'You mean?'

'Is all this really our problem, Paul? What are we doing here? Shouldn't we just get out?'

'And go home and cultivate our gardens? Sniff the roses?'

'Yes.'

'The idea has its attractions.'

'I question the value of what we do, Paul.'

'Don't we all?'

'I mean it, Paul. The world is changing and we've got to change with it.'

'These are dangerous thoughts, Gareth.'

'I know. But I'm thinking them.'

◇◇◇

As Owen went into his office, McPhee was entering his. He had someone with him. A boy.

'Not him again!'

It was the boy from the Helwan races.

'I thought we'd told him to go home!'

'He's going home. He wants to speak to you first.'

'Well, all right,' said Owen resignedly.

The boy came shyly into his office.

'Hello, Yacoub.'

'Effendi!'

Unexpectedly he offered to shake hands; unexpectedly, because it was a Western thing to do.

They shook hands and Owen motioned to him to sit down. The boy remained standing.

'I have not changed my mind,' he said defiantly.

'No?'

'No. But the people I was sent to the City to help have. The Great Sheikh has.'

'Sayed Ali?'

'Yes.'

'How do you know this?'

'The people I was with have been told. At first there was debate about this, because some said one thing, others another. But now the Sheikh himself has spoken.'

'And what did he say?'

'He said that the task was not to shout the walls down but to build. But others said that this was not a time for building but for destroying. Not for planting trees but for cutting them down. But the Great Sheikh said that we should take care when we destroy that we do not destroy good.'

He looked at Owen.

'That was what you told me, Effendi.'

'Well, well, it seems we think alike, the Great Sheikh and I.'

'He said also that we should go back to our places and work to see that good comes of things we now think evil. That, too, Effendi, was what you said.'

'We grow old together, old and wise, the Sheikh and I.'

'I do not agree with the Sheikh. I think we should fight to uproot the bad. But the Sheikh has spoken and what he says must be right.'

'Well—'

'It must be so,' the boy insisted, 'for the Sheikh has risen from his bed to say this. Could so sick and aged a man have risen, if God had not decreed it?'

'Perhaps you will say this to your own sheikh back at the village?'

'I will say it: although whether he will hear me is a different matter.'

'Nevertheless, say it. And do what Sayed Ali bids. Work to see that good comes of ill.'

'I will do that. Effendi. But...'

◇◇◇

So now Owen understood why the procession had not been chanting Sayed Ali's name. The game had changed. The kind of religious uprising had receded. Admittedly, it had been replaced by the threat of more straight forwardly political protest, but that would be easier to deal with. He would have to tell Paul. It might be helpful to him for his tactical manoeuvring.

But what else did it mean? He had been coming to the conclusion that the obscure group around Prince Hamid, who were obviously working for something, and always certainly against the Khedive, and against the British, come to that, had been trying to enlist Sayed Ali in their cause. Their attempt seems to have failed. What would they try next?

◇◇◇

Miss Skiff came to see him.

'Why, Miss Skiff, how good to see you! Is there anything I can do to help you?'

'I have been thinking,' said Miss Skiff.

'Oh, yes?'

'And worrying.'

'About the horses? I really don't think you need to. They are, I gather, in fine fettle.'

'Not about the horses.'

'No?'

'About myself and about that bomb. And wondering if I myself should take some of the responsibility for it.'

'You, Miss Skiff?'

'It was constructed on chemical principles, involving, as I remember you telling me, the interaction of picric and nitric acid. You would not need a lot of scientific knowledge to do that but you would need some. It is the sort of thing an intelligent school boy could put together, the product of a lab and not of a factory. Now, Captain Owen, over the years I have myself taught many intelligent school boys the principles which could have been used.'

'I really don't see how you could blame yourself—'

'Think about it. There are not many schools in Egypt where science is taught. Certainly not to an advanced level. Many of the few who know about science will have been to Victoria College, which, as you know, is the school to which many educated people in Egypt send their sons and where I myself taught science for thirty-six years.'

'I see your line of reasoning, Miss Skiff. But, you know, you haven't taught for some years now and any influence you may have had will have been long since dissipated.'

'Little you know about education, Captain Owen!' snorted Miss Skiff.

'And isn't your responsibility confined, anyway, to giving your pupils knowledge? What use they make of it afterwards is their responsibility not yours.'

'Is it?' said Miss Skiff. 'That is what I have been asking myself.'

'You know, Miss Skiff,' said Owen gently, 'I think that perhaps you take too much responsibility on yourself.'

'Someone has to.'

'Yes, but I think it is best if it is taken for things near one and not at too general a level. Your work for animals, for example, seems to me splendid. But to feel a general responsibility for everything taught in school—'

'Ah!' said Miss Skiff. 'But you don't quite understand. In this case the responsibility is not general. It is particular. I used to include in my course a lesson on explosions—always very popular with the boys. One of the examples I used was the effects of combining picric acid with nitric acid. Hillal reminded me of it yesterday. We had been watching explosives and Hillal suddenly remembered that lesson. And if Hillal remembered it, perhaps someone else did, too.'

◇◇◇

In the hammam the caged birds were singing sweetly. Recumbent forms were lying everywhere on the marble slabs. Some had pulled the screens across and from behind them came the subdued chatter of men either conducting their business or relaxing afterwards. The chatter in any case was almost lost in the continuous bubble and splash of the fountains. The fountains played into a large sunken depression in the centre of the room and men sat about on its edge, their feet dangling in the water. Around them graceful Moorish arches receded in all directions, some of them carrying the main dome, others the minor ones over the marble liwans and over the smaller baths. And everywhere men in loin cloths stooped over the recumbent forms and there was a kind of continuous staccato of cracking joints.

One of the recumbent forms was that of Georgiades. The Greek came now to the hammam every day and spent so much time there that Nikos had been moved to protest.

'You're not paid for just lying there,' he complained.

'Oh, but I am, I am!' said Georgiades. 'And it's a lovely way of earning a living.'

'Life,' beamed the m'allim, 'at least in my hammam, is a bed of roses.'

'Take care,' said Owen, 'that among the roses there may not be thorns.'

The m'allim looked rather put out.

'What thorns was the Effendi thinking of?'

Owen did not reply but continued to wander through the different rooms of the hammam.

'What is the Effendi seeking?' asked the m'allim, following him around uneasily.

'I am just waiting,' said Owen.

Georgiades, not a pretty sight, came through from the harara, wrapped in towels and dripping with perspiration.

Two men had just come into the meslakh. He nodded to them and then went on through to the beyt-owwal to dress.

The m'allim went up to the men and spoke to them. He did that to everyone who came in. He took their valuables and put them in a locker, saw that the lawingi had stored away their clothes and shoes, and then directed them on into the harara, where he assigned them a slab, saw that someone was attending to them, looked around the room to make sure that all was in order, and then went back to the reception room.

The two men who had just come in did not, however, seem to want to make use of the hammam's services. After talking to the m'allim they went out again.

Owen followed them.

They went to a cart loaded with vegetables, the aubergines, tomatoes, and onions that the Egyptians loved. As they were about to climb up into it Owen stopped them.

'Where is it this time?' he asked.

The men looked at him stupidly.

'The message,' he said. 'Where have you to take the message this time?'

'We take many messages.'

'The m'allim's message.'

'*Did* the m'allim give us a message?'

'Yes,' said Owen. 'As he usually does. Now that Hussein and Ahmet are not taking them.'

'We know nothing about this,' said the men uneasily.

'Oh, but you do,' said Owen. 'I saw the m'allim giving you a message. And you have been taking many messages for him lately. You have been watched.'

'There is nothing wrong with taking messages,' said one of the men.

'It depends what the messages are,' said Owen. 'Tell me about the message that the m'allim has just given you to take.'

Georgiades suddenly appeared behind the two men and took them by the arms.

'Tell him,' he said.

'I know what message you have been taking lately,' Owen said. 'Did it not concern Sayed Ali?'

'What if it did?' muttered one of the men.

'Tell me.'

'They are not to come out for Sayed Ali now,' said one of the men unwillingly.

'What are they to do?'

'Some are to go home, others are to hold themselves in readiness.'

'For what?'

'Things have changed. It will not be as was planned.'

'So what will it be?'

'Effendi, we do not know.'

'You will have to do better than that.'

Georgiades tightened his grip on their arms and shook them.

'This is the Mamur Zapt,' he said. 'Tell him.'

'Effendi, we truly do not know.'

'No?'

'But—'

'But?'

'Something is to happen. We do not know what it is. But it will be something that all will remark. And applaud. And when it happens it will be a signal.'

'For what?'

'We do not know, Effendi. No one has yet been told. They have been told only to hold themselves in readiness. When the thing that is to happen, happens, then people will be told.'

'And you have no idea what this thing is?'

'No, Effendi.'

'Do you know when it is to happen?'

'Thursday, Effendi. So that it should not fall on the Sabbath.'

'Because it is a bad deed?'

'We do not know, Effendi.'

Owen turned to Georgiades.

'Take them to the Bab-el-Khalk,' he said, 'and find out from them all the people to whom they have delivered messages in the last few days.'

◇◇◇

Owen went back into the hammam. The m'allim came forward to meet him.

'What is your will, Effendi? A fine bath? A soothing massage?'

'Like the one you had Yussef give to Ziki?'

The m'allim gasped.

'Effendi—'

'Take me somewhere where we can talk.'

The m'allim led him to a small store room used for stacking towels. There was no window and it was very hot.

'Effendi, you should not say such things!'

'I say them because they are true.'

'Effendi, I did not know this Yussef?'

'Why, then, did you employ him?'

'I needed another man, Effendi. To do the massaging.'

'That is not what you told your lawingi. You said there was no need of another man. And then you employed Yussef.'

'I changed my mind.'

'That is true, perhaps. But why did you change your mind?'

'Effendi, I—'

'Shall I tell you? Because someone approached you. Perhaps they gave you money. They said: "Take this man into your service. It will not be for long."'

'No man came!'

'Did he tell you to see that Ziki was served by Yussef?'

'Effendi, I—'

'Speak the truth. You did not speak the truth before when I asked you who had spoken for Yussef when you employed him. You said that Muhammed Ridwan had spoken for him and it was not so. Now that lie will count against you. Do not add to it other lies.'

'Effendi, it is true that a man approached me but I do not know his name.'

'Was he the man who came to you and asked you to deliver messages?'

'Effendi, I know nothing about such messages—'

'I think you do. Did you not get Hussein and Ahmet to deliver them for you? Messages, among other things, which, too, will count against you. And now, with Hussein and Ahmet gone, you have asked other carriers to deliver for you. They are in my hands and I have talked to them. So do not move from the truth.'

'It—it may be as you say, Effendi.'

'And was the man who asked you to deliver the messages the same man as the one who asked you to take Yussef into your service?'

'No, Effendi.'

'No?'

'No. I speak the truth, Effendi.'

'It was not the same man?'

'No, Effendi.'

'Who was it, then?'

'Ziki, Effendi.'

'I thought you said you did not know him? When we looked at his body?'

'Well—'

'Never mind, for the moment. Ziki was the one who asked you to deliver messages?'

'Yes, Effendi. And he it was who first asked Hussein and Ahmet to deliver them.'

'And the package?'

'And the package, Effendi.'

'Why did he not deliver them himself? Since he was a carrier, too?'

'There were so many messages, Effendi. He delivered some himself but could not deliver all.'

'So, then, it was another man who came to you about Yussef and who told you to see that he was assigned to tend Ziki?'

'Yes, Effendi.'

'And you do not know his name?'

'No, Effendi.'

'But you knew him?'

The m'allim nodded mutely.

'You know him because he has been to the hammam himself?'

'That is so, Effendi,' the m'allim muttered.

'Was he the one who came with Ziki? The man with fine clothes, who looked on people as if they were ants?'

'That is the man, Effendi.'

'The man smelling of roses?'

◇◇◇

The effects of the changes in the High Commissioner's security dispositions were not apparent at first sight. Owen continued to take direct responsibility for the Commission's security, and British soldiers began to flood on to the streets only slowly. But flood they did, and after a while people began to notice.

'I protest,' said Zaghlul.

'It's no good protesting to me,' said Owen.

Zaghlul gave him a sharp look.

'So that's how it is, is it?' he said, giving Owen a friendly clap on the shoulder.

Zaghlul had been giving evidence to the Commission for almost two days now and, understandably, was looking weary. More than weary, drained. Even before his deportation to Malta he had not looked well and on his return Owen had been shocked at this deterioration.

As he left the room after giving his evidence he stumbled and would have fallen if Owen had not caught him.

'It is nothing,' he said, brushing the incident aside.

But Owen thought it was something and insisted on taking him to the hospital for a check-up.

He took him in his (Owen's) car.

'Hah!' said Zaghlul, looking at it. 'Privilege everywhere!'

'Temporary only,' said Owen. 'I have to give it back next week.'

Zaghlul said nothing further, which was unlike him. Owen had always got on well with the Leader of the Opposition. He respected his prickly independence.

When they got to the hospital Cairns-Grant was, fortunately, there and piloted Zaghlul in to a series of tests.

Coming down the corridor was Zeinab.

'What!' said Zaghlul, aghast. 'A woman! And an Englishman in charge!' he added, looking at Cairns-Grant.

'Aye,' said Cairns-Grant, 'and lucky for you, with all my best men away.'

'Where are they?'

'Abroad. Picking up knowledge which they can then pass on to Egypt.'

Zaghlul snorted.

'And, incidentally,' said Cairns-Grant. 'I'm not English. I'm a Scot.'

Zaghlul, who knew Cairns-Grant of old, laughed.

'Another oppressed people!' he said.

Owen went back to his office. Just before he went home at the end of the day, a letter arrived from Zaghlul, thanking him for his help. He said that the tests had shown that he was diabetic.

'Cairns-Grant assures me,' he said, 'that it can be treated and should not hinder me in any political career, provided I am sensible. "You will be able." he told me, "to continue as a thorn in the flesh of everyone for years to come."'

◇◇◇

Miriam had taken to being Zeinab's assistant like a duck to water. She loved every minute of her job. Nevertheless, she was seriously wondering whether she should go on with it.

The problem was not her but her brother. Asif had not said anything to her about her work in the hospital since his encounter with Miss Skiff but she thought he had gone on brooding about it. He seemed very cast down and Miriam could only conclude that it was because of her. She had expected anger and opposition but not this depression. Open hostility she had anticipated and was prepared, indignantly, to fight against. But not this sudden broken-downness, this near-collapse. She loved her brother and could not bear to see him like this. She knew how seriously he regarded his family duties and felt the weight of the responsibility left on him by the death of his father. She did not want to add to the burden placed on his shoulders but knew that she had.

Did she not have responsibilities too? Was not the burden left by the death of their father to be carried on her shoulders too?

She went to see Zeinab and said that, much as she loved her work, she would have to give it up.

Zeinab put her pencil down.

'Are you sure about this? she said. 'I would miss you greatly.'

'And I, you,' said Miriam. 'I am so—so grateful to you for giving me a chance.'

'Then why give it up?'

Miriam hesitated.

'It is my brother,' she said at last. 'I know him and know that it is weighing on him heavily.'

'But, Miriam,' said Zeinab, 'there are other responsibilities, too. To yourself, for instance. You should not give up everything just for your brother. You have a duty to yourself as well. And—and to other women in the same position as you. Didn't you say that, yourself? Haven't we agreed on that?'

'We have, Zeinab, and I feel terrible about it!'

Miriam burst into tears.

Zeinab didn't quite know how to handle this. She was herself a very self-contained person. She had always, in a way, had to stand on her own. She had never really known her mother or been able to draw on the support of family. Nuri, she knew, cared for her deeply but that was not the same thing. This was a kind of emotional intimacy that she had never known.

And so she did not know now how to handle Miriam's tears. In a funny way she was more used to men crying. And men were often more labile in their emotions and were prepared to demonstrate them in public. They habitually put their arms around each other. She knew that her husband was still slightly disconcerted by this. He was quite prepared to put arms around her, even in public, which she herself, Zeinab, found rather shocking. Men, yes, but men and women? Faintly lewd at best, certainly immodest; and absolutely, impossibly, sexually explosive. Such behaviour should be kept for the house. Even Zeinab, who considered herself extremely liberated, felt this.

And now this crying!

Zeinab put her arms around Miriam. It seemed the right thing to do.

Miriam continued to sob against her for some time and then withdrew.

'I am sorry,' she said.

'Of course you can give it up if you want to,' Zeinab said. 'But think it over first.'

Miriam got back to her forms and Zeinab, after a little internal shrug, did likewise. After a while she was able to think of a reason why she should go and call in on one of the labs.

◇◇◇

Zeid stuck his head in at the door and said that the boy, Salah, had something he wanted to tell him.

Salah entered beaming.

It had happened, he said. Something beyond his wildest dreams. He had been allowed to sit in the front seat of the De Dion and get his hands on the wheel.

And he owed it all, the driver said, to Prince Hamid. Hamid—at last—had seen him hanging around and had asked the driver who the hell was that boy? The driver had apologised—they would kick the boy out on the instant, they had always had it in mind—but they had let him hang around because he was so keen on the cars, the De Dion especially.

'Really?' said Prince Hamid thoughtfully. 'Really?' Then he had laughed. 'Well,' he had said, 'he shows good taste!' And he had told the driver not to kick him out but to let him get behind the wheel. 'Give him a run,' he had said, 'around the courtyard.'

The driver had done that. He had done it more than once. He had gone further. He had shown Salah where to put his hands and feet and had laughed indulgently when Salah had had difficulties in reaching the pedals. The Prince had laughed too. 'Give him a couple of blocks!' he had said, 'so that his feet can get down there. Then—' and this was what Salah now told Owen with bated breath—'he'll really be able to drive it.'

Yes—he had said that! 'Really be able to drive it.' And the driver had said he would teach him, since that seemed to be what Prince Hamid wished. So that in years to come—years, mind you, as there was much to be learned—Salah might even aspire to be assistant to one of the Prince's drivers.

Salah was ecstatic.

Very nice, said Owen, but what about the job to which Owen had assigned him? What about the two men who had come to the water-cart depot? Had Salah talked to the driver of the De Dion? Had he found out who the two men were?

Oh, yes, said Salah airily, his mind now on other things. Definitely not the place to take a De Dion to. Hordes of urchins eager to get their filthy paws on the bodywork he had polished so lovingly. It would have been better if he had been allowed to take the car right into the depot. But the two men had insisted that he stop outside and wait for them.

'And their names,' prompted Owen? 'Had he been able to find out the names of the two men?'

One of them was a lowly man, said the driver, not fit to ride in a De Dion. He had been hanging around the Prince lately, doing his errands, and seemed to have come to him with the other man. His name was Ziki.

And the other man? A different kettle of fish entirely. A man who knew his De Dions. and, apparently, his princes, too.

Certainly, he had known the Prince in the past, although he had only recently swum again into view. The prince had greeted him as an old friend and had made much of him. Too much, in the driver's view; the fellow gave himself airs. But you couldn't complain, as he was so much in the Prince's counsels.

'And his name,' asked Owen?

The driver had never really grasped his name. The Prince seemed to make a point of not using it, and it was not a thing you could ask. But he must be a Pasha's son at least, for the Prince to treat him with such familiarity.

Chapter Twelve

The Parquet had got its man. Yussef had been arrested. It had happened as Sadiq, the Parquet officer in charge of the case, had suggested it would. The masseurs of Cairo were a tight-knit group, operating almost as a guild. Yussef had come from outside, from Assouan, deep in the south of Egypt, and had been regarded as an interloper. He was a good masseur and, once he had been tried, had had no difficulty in getting patients. But the patients had been private ones. He had found it difficult to get employment at any of the public hammams. Private patients were not easily found, and certainly not so easily found as to make it unnecessary for him to engage in what his fellows discounted as 'dubious practices.'

To add to his problems, he had come to Cairo with something of a record. He had been obliged to leave Assouan in a hurry because of an incident that had happened. Someone had died.

This had not endeared him to his fellow practitioners. In addition to the damage the employment of such fellows caused to the reputation of such an honourable profession, it made the other masseurs rather afraid of him; and therefore not at all unwilling to betray to the Parquet his present whereabouts.

He was now being held by the police in a caracol down by the Khan-el-Khalil, the great bazaar area of Cairo. Sadiq had at once notified Mahmoud, as he had said he would, and had proposed that they go down together to question him.

As they were arriving, another arabeah drew up outside the caracol. Out of it stepped Mr. Narwat.

'Another client for you, Mr. Narwat?' said Mahmoud.

'Yes, indeed,' said Mr. Narwat. 'And if you are going to interview him, I am afraid I must insist on your doing it in my presence.'

Sadiq was faintly surprised. He knew by repute of Mr. Narwat and of the fees he charged and had not expected to find him employed by an out-of-work masseur such as Yussef.

Yussef, it turned out, was also surprised. He was a squat, surly thick-set fellow whom even without knowing his record, many hammams would not happily employ. When Mr. Narwat introduced himself, he viewed him with suspicion.

'Lawyer?' he said. 'I don't have a lawyer.'

'You do now,' said Mr. Narwat winningly.

'Nor do I want one,' said Yussef.

'Maybe,' said Mr. Narwat. 'But you're going to need one.'

Yussef spat on the floor.

'I don't like lawyers,' he said.

'Nevertheless...'

'You bugger off,' said Yussef, turning his back on him.

'I am the Parquet officer in charge of the case,' said Sadiq, 'and I would like to ask you a few questions.'

'And you can bugger off, too,' said Yussef belligerently.

'Your name is Yussef?'

'Who's saying it's not?'

'And you were employed at the hammam in Shafik Street?'

'My client does not have to answer that question,' interrupted Mr. Narwat.

'Oh,' said Mahmoud, 'but he is not your client. I distinctly heard him say so. You can proceed,' he said to Sadiq.

'Just a minute—' said Mr. Narwat.

'Between the following dates,' continued Sadiq.

'I don't know much about dates,' said Yussef, 'but anyone will tell you when I was employed there.'

'Yussef...' began Mr. Narwat.

'And they also knew what happened there,' said Yussef. 'I broke his neck.'

'I really must insist—'

'Is this man employed by you?' Mahmoud asked Yussef.

'Employed?' said Yussef, astonished. 'Me? Look, I don't employ anybody. I'm a free man and I treat other people as free men. I'm not one of those people who own others. Nor would I want to be.'

'I would advise you, I really would *strongly* advise you—' began Mr. Narwat.

'Piss off!' said Yussef.

'You heard!' said Mahmoud.

'In my client's interests—'

'He is *not* your client,' said Sadiq. 'He has several times said so. In view of that, Mr. Narwat, I must ask you to withdraw.'

'Well!' said Mr. Narwat.

Mahmoud accompanied him out.

'Are you sure you're backing the right horse?' he said.

'What do you mean?' said Mr. Narwat.

'The Khedive is taking a personal interest in this case,' said Mahmoud. 'Not surprisingly, since it concerns him. And he has the support of the Parquet and of the Ministry of Justice. Not to mention the British. Are you wise to allow yourself to be associated with a group which has attempted to blow up the Khedive and also clearly been responsible for a murder committed by this man?'

'My duty as a lawyer—'

'Just think about it,' said Mahmoud.

He smiled and patted Mr. Narwat on the shoulder.

'Oh, and just think what you will say when the Parquet formally asks you to divulge the name of the person that has employed you.'

'I have a duty of confidentiality—'

'Just think about it,' said Mahmoud. 'But think very hard.'

◇◇◇

He went back in to where Sadiq was questioning Yussef. Yussef was being surprisingly forthcoming.

'I don't give a toss now,' he said, 'now that I've got the money.'

'It won't do you much good,' said Sadiq.

'Ah,' said Yussef, 'but that's not the point.'

'What is the point, then, Yussef?' asked Sadiq, surprised.

'Ah!' said Yussef.

'Is it that it will do someone else some good?' asked Mahmoud.

Now it was Yussef who looked surprised.

'You're a sharp bugger, aren't you?' he said to Mahmoud. 'Who is it?'

'I'm not telling you,' said Yussef. 'Otherwise you might take the money back.'

'We might not want it back,' said Mahmoud. 'Not if you were helpful enough.'

Yussef looked tempted, then shook his head.

'Na-ow,' he said. 'I know you lot. I wouldn't trust you an inch.'

'We might find out anyway,' said Mahmoud. 'Now that we've found you, we'll go back to everyone who knows you. And if we find out that way, then you certainly won't keep the money. Who is she?'

Yussef looked staggered.

'She?' he repeated. 'You crafty sod. How did you know?'

'We know quite a lot about you, Yussef.'

Yussef looked worried.

'Look,' he said, 'I don't want you lot blundering in and making a mess of things.'

'We don't need to blunder in. Not if you tell us what we have to know.'

Yussef hesitated.

Mahmoud and Sadiq waited.

'All right, then,' he said suddenly. 'It's for my mother.'

'Your mother!' said both Mahmoud and Sadiq, amazed.

'Yes. I want her to have this money. And not all in one go, or else she'll give it all to the mosque. I want it in dribs and drabs, when she needs it, like, and I've set this up. So she'll be all right no matter what happens to me. I'm in for it, anyway, and would be, some time or other, even if it wasn't for this. So I've to think ahead, and now I have done, and set it up. You see, there's no one else that'll look after her. Now that my father's gone. Not that he would have done anything for her. A right old bastard, he was. That was why I killed him.'

'You killed him?'

'Yes. One day he went too far. He always used to beat her. Used to beat me, too, but I could stand it. She couldn't. And one day he went too far when he was beating her and I heard something snap. I was a masseur, right? And I knew what it meant. So I got hold of him—he was a big man, but I'm bigger—and I said: "That's enough!" "I'll bloody kill you!" he said. "You won't," I said.

'And I killed him. Pulled his neck out, just like you do with chickens. Of course, that meant I had to get out, which I did. But that meant I had to leave her without anything much, and I didn't like that, because she always used to stand up for me. That's usually how she got her beatings. So I said: "I've got to go now, but one day I'll make it all right for you." So when this bloke came along, I thought this was my chance.'

'When this bloke came along?'

'That's right. Funny that was. He was in a car, see. A big, posh car. Now, I don't hold with cars, and I don't hold much with the people who drive them, either. They've always got more money than is good for them. So when he knocked Ali over, I went up to him and said: "I'm going to stretch your neck." And he looked at me, as cool as you like, and said: "No need to." He looked at Ali. "He'll be all right," he said, and gave me some money. "That'll see to him," he said.

'Then he turned back to me. "You seem an amiable fellow," he said. That was the way he talked. All la-de-dah. But nasty "You're right," I said. "And to show you, I think I'll tie your neck in a knot." "That's no way to get on in the world," he said. "I can show you a better."

'Well, I didn't take to him, and that's the truth. I wanted to have nothing to do with him. But he looked at me, as cool as

you like, and said: "Come with me, my man." My man! That's
what he said. If that wasn't enough to make me want to wring
his neck...

'He just looked at me and said: "You're a brute. And I could
just do with a brute." "You'll have to do without me," I said.
"Oh?" he said. And named a sum.

'When I got my breath back I said: "What do I have to do
for this?" "Wring a neck," he said.

'Well, I thought about it. It was a lot of money. A lot! So I
said: "Tell me about it." But he wouldn't tell me about it at first,
he asked me lots of questions. And when I said I was a masseur,
he said: "That'll do very nicely." And he upped the money.'

He shrugged.

'Well, that's it,' he said. 'He offered me the money, and I took
it. And I've arranged things so that it will all go to my mother.'

'And Ziki?' asked Sadiq.

'Ziki?'

'The man you killed.'

Yussef shrugged.

'He's dead,' he said.

◇◇◇

Owen meanwhile had been talking to Ziki's widow. He found her
not at her house but up outside the prison talking to the carter.

'Effendi?'

'We have talked before.'

She nodded.

'I know,' she said.

He looked at the cart.

'You still have the prison contract, then?'

'We do, God be praised.'

'You have had it a long time.'

'Not long. It came to us after Ziki was released from prison.'

'As a reward?'

'It was said that it was out of kindness, but Ziki said it was
for keeping his mouth shut.'

'About what?'

She hesitated.

'There was some foolishness. The Pasha's son was part of it, and so was Prince Hamid. Ziki was not part of it but they used him and he knew things. The prison contract was to stop his mouth. The Pasha's son arranged it with the Palace.'

'With the Palace?'

'There was someone there who could arrange such things. He worked on the purchasing side and had been, well, one of those who were with Prince Hamid.'

'His name?'

'Asif.'

It was the name that Owen had paused over when Nikos had presented to him the list of the people who had been part of Prince Hamid's group.

Owen nodded.

'And he arranged it?'

'Yes. The Pasha's son went to him. It was in the days when the Pasha's son smiled on us.'

'And did he not continue, then, to smile?'

'We heard nothing of him for months. And I said: "He has forgotten us." But Ziki said: "Perhaps it is better thus." For he had not liked some of the things he had been called on to do when he was with them. And we thought no more of it. But then the Pasha's son came to him again. And this time Ziki did not want to go with him. "Last time," he said, "it was prison. What will it be this time?" And he tried to say that to the Pasha's son, and the Pasha's son was angry. "You are part of my design," he said. "What do you think I got you the carrier business for?" He said it would go hard with him if he did not do as he was told.

'So Ziki began to work for him again. But he did not like it. And one day he came to me and said: "This is terrible. I cannot do as he asks." Nevertheless, he had to do it. He was, you see, still a bound man to the Pasha. Bound in his heart, although he had left him years before.

'Even so, as time went on, he became more and more unhappy. His heart rebelled. And one day he said to me: "Let us sell the business and go to Assiut, and I will find work there." But I counseled him, God forgive me, to wait. "Wait until the Pasha's business is done," I said. "And then he will go away as before and leave us alone."

'And Ziki did as I advised. But he said: "Ill will come of this." And I said, "Never mind that, as long as it does not come on us." But Ziki said, "I know too much. He will not try to shut my mouth with gold this time."'

◇◇◇

Mahmoud told Owen that Mr. Narwat had decided to withdraw from the case.

'He is no longer going to represent Yussef?'

'Nor Hussein and Ahmet. He senses, I think, which way the wind is blowing.'

'Ah!' said Owen, and went to see Hussein and Ahmet. This time he had the two water-cart drivers brought in together.

'Ziki is dead,' he said. 'You are not. This is because you are safe in prison.'

'Ziki is dead?'

They had not known, and the news shook them.

'Those who know too much,' said Owen, 'have their mouths stopped. You, also, know too much.'

He let them ponder it.

'He will do to you as he did to Ziki. Unless you tell me what I want to know.'

◇◇◇

Zeinab had been disturbed by what Zaghlul had said when he saw her in the hospital. 'A woman!' he had registered, with horror. She had been surprised at this. Zaghlul was a cultivated man, quite Westernised, she had thought, one of those whom Mahmoud would have considered 'modern.' She knew him slightly—he had never been an intimate of her father, but they had met occasionally at functions, and she had always felt that she got on with him. But she did not like this.

Over the next day or two she had found herself thinking about it increasingly. If Zaghlul, the astute, sophisticated leader of the Wafd party, the man who, her husband assured her, could still become the next Prime Minister, thought like this, how would others be thinking? If they thought the same, how would she fare in this new Egypt that they all thought they would be building?

Since their dinner with Mahmoud and Aisha she had been thinking a lot about politics and the future of their country. She had never thought about it much before, assuming, supreme realist that she was, that things would go on much the same. The assumption of Mahmoud and Aisha that things would not go on the same had rather intrigued her. It had made her consider where she herself stood.

And where did she stand? She wasn't quite sure. Of course she was Egyptian. But she didn't seem to be Egyptian in quite the way other people were. In the way that Mahmoud and Aisha were, for instance. They felt passionately about Egypt. They identified, yes, that was it, they identified themselves with Egypt much more than she did.

She knew that this was partly, probably, largely, to do with her upbringing. She had been brought up in a Pasha's household and the Pashas had always been somehow distant from the rest of the population. It was a question of lords and serfs. But it was more than that. The Pashas, with their wealth and freedom, had always looked outwards. And usually they had looked to France.

Not so much to England. Perhaps they had fewer illusions about the British, since they were dealing with them on a day-to-day basis. In a way they despised them. They considered them, with their heavy boots and stiff manners, inferior culturally to themselves and certainly to the French. It was to France that the Egyptian ruling class looked for their culture, their clothes, and their entertainment. It was to Cannes, not Blackpool, that they went for their holidays (understandably); Paris, not London, that they looked for their styles.

Nuri, intending the best for his daughter, had brought Zeinab up like this. The result was that she shared the cosmopolitan outlook of the privileged Egyptian rich and had never been greatly in touch with what went on below. She, like the Pasha class as a whole, had grown away from Egypt; and what she was suddenly coming to realise was that this might do her, and them, no good.

But this separation was not a complete thing. In many ways she still felt intensely Egyptian; particularly when it came to injustices inflicted on Egypt by other countries. So she was quite drawn to the vision Mahmoud painted of an independent Egypt staying true to its roots but going its own way. That was how she saw herself, too: independent, going her own way, but still somehow true to herself as an Egyptian.

But now she was beginning to ask herself if that was the way that others saw her. And the question came to a head over this business of being a woman. Zeinab was no suffragette. She was aware of what was going on in Europe and applauded the movement towards a new definition of women. But there didn't seem much point in bothering about a vote for women when no one in Egypt had the vote. But she was very bothered about other things affecting the place of women. Work, for instance.

She had loved going out to work and to work in the hospital. She realised she had a talent for it and that it fulfilled her in unexpected ways. She had come to think that she had a right to it. Why shouldn't she do a job like this? And if her, why not other women? Miriam's coming had made a difference to her way of thinking. Yes, why not? she had found herself asking. And she had been disappointed at Miriam's wanting to give it up.

There was definitely a place for women in interesting jobs in Zeinab's new Egypt; but was there a place for women in interesting jobs in Zaghlul's new Egypt? That was the question that was worrying her.

And then suddenly there flashed into her mind a new consideration, one that had never entered her thinking before: what if—the question of a baby had never quite slipped out of her thoughts—she had a baby and it turned out to be a daughter?

Zeinab didn't know much about babies but she did know that roughly half of them did turn out to be girls and she thought it possible that it might be true in her case. If that was so then it put a completely new complexion on things. She was prepared to take her chances when it came to herself, but for her daughter she wanted only the best.

This bore thinking about.

◇◇◇

Owen had been brought a message from Paul. The Commission had received a sudden invitation to a Royal Reception at the Abdin Palace the next day. Paul regarded this as a triumph, since the Khedive had hitherto refused to acknowledge the presence of the Commission, declaring its existence an infringement of Egypt's sovereign rights. Now, however, after much lobbying by Paul, he appeared to have changed his mind.

There was, however, a problem. Under the High Commissioner's new dispositions, while Owen as Mamur Zapt was responsible for the personal security of the members of the Commission, the Army had taken over a general responsibility for the situation in the streets. To get them from their hotel to the Palace the Commission had to pass through the streets; and the Army proposed to safeguard their security by lining the streets with troops.

Paul did not think this was a good idea. Nor, more to the point, did the Khedive. After what had happened on his most recent attempt to process, he had gone off the idea of procession. Even when it was somebody else who was processing. In any case he took umbrage over the Army playing a role in all this. As far as he was concerned, the Mamur Zapt had always been responsible for the realm's—and his—security and he saw no reason to change this. The presence of the British Army was, somewhat heroically, another of the things he refused to recognise.

It was agreed that the Commission should proceed to the Palace in cars sent by the Khedive. Not in procession, but with

Owen driving with them, in his very own car. It was probably the last opportunity he would have of using it before he had to give it back.

He arranged for the car to pick him up at the Bab-el-Khalk the next day.

◇◇◇

Asif was so deeply depressed that he even stayed away from work. This had never happened before and Miriam was disturbed. She believed it all her fault. If she had not insisted on going out to work, this would not have happened. Asif had locked himself away in his room. Plucking up her courage, Miriam knocked timidly at this door. When there was no reply, she knocked again.

The door was flung open.

'Cannot I be left alone?' demanded Asif.

'I wanted to tell you something,' Miriam said falteringly.

'Tell me some other time. Cannot you see that I am sick?'

'It is because you are sick that I wanted to tell you this,' said Miriam bravely. 'I thought it would help.'

Now it was Asif's heart that smote. She seemed so modest and submissive. Could it be that she was returning to a proper sense of dutifulness?

He had not behaved well to his sister. He had failed in his own duties as head of the household. Surely he could at least listen to her?

He stood back and let her enter.

'Speak on,' he said.

'I thought—I thought you were unhappy with me,' she said.

'Well, I am.'

'But it's all right. I am going to stop. I am not going to work at the hospital any more.'

'Not?' said Asif, surprised.

'Not. If it makes you so unhappy.'

'Well—'

'And ill.'

'Ill? It's not that that's making me ill!' said Asif.

'Not—?'

'Of course, not! You can do what you want as far as I am concerned.'

What was he saying?

'Provided you conduct yourself in a seemly fashion,' he added hastily.

'But it's not that that's making you ill?'

'No, no.'

'It's something else?'

'Something else, yes.'

'Cannot you tell me, my dear?'

Miriam had never called him that before.

His heart melted.

'I have such terrible troubles,' he muttered. 'Whatever I do I shall bring dishonour and distress upon my family.'

'Tell me,' she insisted.

He found it very hard to tell her. He had always fought his own way, had never wanted, or accepted, help from others. He had always preferred to act alone. When his father had been alive he had gone to him: but that had been not so much to ask for advice but to tell him of his triumphs. He had wanted, needed, his father to be proud of him, and was sure that he had been. But they had never really talked as intimates, as equals, as colleagues, say. And now, when he badly needed to talk to someone, he was not there.

And would he have understood, anyway?

Asif suddenly realised that it was not so much advice that he was in need of as, well…sympathy. He wanted someone who would understand him, be on his side, feel for him and with him, reach out to him…

As his sister had done, in fact.

He broke down in sobs and she put her arms around him.

'I have got it all wrong,' he said. 'Wrong! Wrong! Everything I did was wrong.'

'Nonsense!' said Miriam.

'The way I behaved to you, the way I behaved to other people…the way I behaved to the Khedive…'

'The Khedive?' said Miriam, astounded.

'Yes. Our father served the Khedive loyally all his life. And he brought us up to be loyal servants of the Khedive, too. It was his proudest moment—he told me this—when I joined him at the Palace. And, afterwards, as I moved upwards, he followed everything I did with… It gave him great happiness, he said, to see me fulfilling myself in service to the master he had followed for so many years, all his life.

'And I was proud and happy, too. But then—then I began to meet other people. And they thought differently from the way I did. They said that the Khedive was a weak man, and a bad man, and that what he did was not good for Egypt. That all those things that were wrong with Egypt would not be righted until he was removed. And I listened to them. My eyes were blinded and my mind clouded—'

'What have you done?' said Miriam.

'Pride,' said Asif. 'That's what it was. Among all those rich and powerful people. I wanted to show them that I was as good as they. I had something that they hadn't. Knowledge. I had always been good at school and knew things they did not. I knew about science. About how to make explosives. Bombs. So when they talked about striking a blow, I could tell them how. Miss Skiff, unwittingly, had shown me—yes, and I have betrayed her, too. She gave me knowledge that I could use to do good, yes, to my own country—'

He beat upon his breast.

'I could have used it for Egypt. Instead…'

'What have you done?' said Miriam.

'At the time, it came to nothing. They talked about it and bombs were made, by a foolish technician. But they were never thrown. The police found out and we were all seized. There were powerful men in the group and they had people to speak for them. In the end we were allowed free. Only the foolish technician was punished. He was sent to prison. And I, having been pardoned, buried myself in my work.

'This was all three years ago and I thought belonged to the past. But recently—recently they came to me again and said that they were going to try again, and that the need now was even greater. They asked me to tell again how a bomb might be made, and to explain it again to the man who had made the bombs before. It was the same man and he was no happier than I. But they said, if you do not help, we will reveal all.

'So I helped. I told them. And the bomb was made. It was to be used against the Khedive. It was not to be thrown but to be placed in a water-cart and would explode when the Khedive went past.

'God be praised, it was not exploded. They found out in time. But when I thought about what might have happened—'

'Well, it did not happen,' said Miriam, after a moment. 'And for that, as you say, God must be praised. But there must be no more of this, my brother. I say this in our father's name, there must be no more of this!'

'But there will be,' Asif whispered. 'They are plotting something. I do not know what it is, but I know they intend to strike again. They asked me to join them and this time I refused. Miriam, I am frightened. I fear they may strike at me. I know too much. They have killed one already, that poor man I told you about. I fear that they will do the same to me. But at least I will know that I have refused to lift my hand again against the Khedive.'

'We do not sit here,' said Miriam. 'We do not sit here quietly waiting for the wolf to strike. Come with me.'

◇◇◇

Owen received a phone call from Zeinab asking him to come at once to the hospital.

Owen looked at his watch. He was due at the Commission's hotel in less than an hour to escort them to the Palace. He could just manage it; especially if he went in the car.

As he was leaving the Bab-el-Khalk he ran into Zeid and Salah. They were just coming to see him. Salah wanted to tell him about the latest miracle that had happened to him. Prince Hamid had allowed him to drive the De Dion all by himself. Without even the driver sitting beside him!

'Congratulations!' said Owen. 'You must be doing well.'

'The Prince thinks highly of him,' Zeid said proudly. 'He is always saying what a good driver Salah is going to be.'

'Well, that's tremendous!' said Owen.

'And today he is going to let me drive outside the Palace!' said Salah excitedly.

'I hope that is sensible,' said Owen.

'Oh, it is, it is!' said Salah. 'We are going to the Automobile Club now. And there we will pick up the De Dion and I am going to drive it all on my own. Only a short way. But the Prince says that will be enough.'

'Just be careful, will you?' said Owen, and hurried on.

◇◇◇

Zeinab was waiting anxiously for him at the hospital entrance and took him into her office. He was surprised to see Asif there as well as Miriam.

'Tell him!' commanded Miriam.

Owen listened in silence.

'And they plan to strike again?' he said, when Asif had finished.

'Yes,' said Asif hoarsely.

'Do you know where?'

Asif shook his head.

'He would not tell me,' he said. 'Not after I refused. I know only that it will be a great blow. Even though this time it will not be against the Khedive directly.'

'A great blow?'

'That will make England tremble.'

Owen nodded.

'And this man, this man who spoke to you, what is his name?'

Asif hesitated.

'Tell!' commanded Miriam.

'Does he smell of roses?' asked Owen.

And then suddenly sat up.

'A great blow? England? *England?*

◇◇◇

He leaped from his chair and ran out of the room.

'The Savoy!' he said to the driver. 'Quickly!'

The car skidded out of the hospital grounds.

'Faster!' said Owen. 'You've got to get there faster!'

'Blast!' said the driver.

They had got caught behind a slow-moving ox-drawn cart.

'Overtake!' commanded Owen.

'You really mean that?' said the driver.

He pulled out from behind the cart. An arabeah coming the other way swung violently over. It stopped and its driver stood up shouting imprecations.

The car accelerated. It swung in and out of a whole line of carts, arabeahs, and startled people.

'You did say—' began the driver.

'Get on!' snapped Owen.

As they swerved down the impossibly crowded street stall-holders sprang aside, chickens squawked, and pedestrians turned in amazement.

'I'm going to take us down the Mouski, right?' said the driver. 'And if anyone says anything afterwards, as they will, I'm going to say I was acting under orders.'

'Right!' said Owen.

'If you say so,' said the driver, and put his foot on the pedal.

As they tore along the Mouski they were followed by a grow-ing crescendo of protest. At the end of the street it was joined by police whistles.

A policeman bravely stepped out and held up his hand.

'Keep going!' said Owen.

The policeman sprang aside.

'This has done me,' said the driver.

'I'll see you're all right.'

The car turned at last on to the Sharia Kasr-en-Nil. There, ahead of them, was the Hotel and outside it several cars were drawn up and the members of the Commission getting in.

And there, approaching from the other end of the street, driven slowly and carefully, was the De Dion. With a small boy alone at the wheel.

Chapter Thirteen

Owen jumped out.

'Block the street! Turn the car across the road!'

Paul was standing beside the cars seeing everybody in. He looked up in surprise.

'Get them away!' Owen shouted. 'Bombs! Get them inside!'

Paul ran along the line of cars telling them to drive away. There were soldiers standing nearby and they began to hustle the remaining members of the Commission inside.

'Everyone!' shouted Owen. 'Get everyone away!'

Without looking to see if his orders were being obeyed, he ran up the road towards the De Dion.

It slowed. He could see the figure at the wheel clearly now.

He waved the car down. It came uncertainly to a stop. Owen wrenched open the door.

'Out!' he said. 'Quickly!'

He caught Salah by the collar of his galabeah and hauled him out.

'Run!'

Zeid, appearing suddenly beside him, scooped the boy up in his arms and took off.

Owen wrenched open the rear door. There, on the floor, and on the back seats, was a huge package. He bent over it.

Someone pushed him aside.

'Leave it to us!' said the Sirdar. 'Some things we may not know about but this sort of thing we bloody do!'

He pulled Owen away.

Soldiers were now swarming all over the car.

A cry went up.

'Got it, sir!'

'Just make sure, will you?'

He walked Owen back towards the hotel.

Zeid was standing there still holding Salah in his arms.

'They used the boy, did they?'

Owen looked round and saw Georgiades.

'The man smelling of roses,' he said. 'He may be here.'

Georgiades nodded and rushed off.

'And Hamid!' said Owen. 'I want Prince Hamid. Especially.'

'He's gone to the Palace,' someone said.

'I'm going to get him,' said Owen. 'Where's my car?'

Paul hurried up.

'Okay, now?' he said.

'Okay. They can go to the Palace now. There's no reason why the Reception shouldn't go ahead.'

An officer came up.

'Have you got them?' he said excitedly. 'Do you know who they are?'

'I know who they are,' said Owen.

'You really mean Prince Hamid?' asked the Sirdar.

'I do. There may be some difficulty in getting him. He's at the Palace.'

'I'll come with you,' said the Sirdar. 'There won't be any difficulty then.'

Owen's car had drawn up. They climbed in.

'The Palace,' said Owen.

'Quickly?' said the driver.

'Quickly,' said the Sirdar.

The Sirdar was dressed for Reception. In uniform. Splendidly. And recognisably.

There was no difficulty at the gates. They swung open and the car went through them.

The Sirdar jumped out.

Flunkeys had already assembled to show the Commission's members in.

'Hamid!' said the Sirdar. 'I want Prince Hamid. Where is he?'

'In his rooms, sir. He's not coming to the reception.'

'No, he's not,' said the Sirdar. 'Take me to him.' He turned to Owen. 'You look after the Commission and see they're all right. Explain things to them. Oh, and to the Khedive, too.'

◇◇◇

Explaining to the Commission was easy. They arrived at the Palace looking somewhat bemused and after Paul had assembled them Owen had a word with them before they went in.

'You mean,' said Mrs. Oliphant, looking thoughtful, 'there was a bomb in that car coming down the road toward us?'

'Dynamite,' said Owen, 'and a slow burning fuse. Already lit.'

'But was not that a small boy I saw driving the car?'

'It was.'

'Hum,' said Mrs. Oliphant, looking even more thoughtful.

◇◇◇

The Khedive, addressed privately at the end of the Reception, was thoughtful, too.

'Hamid has always been a problem,' he said.

'I think, Your Highness, that it would be better if he were less in circulation.'

'You know,' said the Khedive, 'that idea has occurred to me, too.'

'I will look after his unpleasant friends, and I don't think they're likely to be a problem for quite some time. But Prince Hamid—'

The Khedive smiled.

'Leave it to me,' he said. 'I will see that he is less in circulation in future. Yes, very much less.'

He patted Owen familiarly on the shoulder.

'Oh, and it has not escaped my notice, Mamur Zapt,' he said, 'that twice in the last month you have foiled assassination

attempts, not least against my own person. I hope you are thinking of staying around?'

◇◇◇

Zeid was waiting for Owen when he left. He had a message
from Georgiades. Would Owen join him as soon as possible?
Zeid had the address.

The house was a small one in the Ismailiya, a well-to-do
quarter of Cairo. Georgiades was waiting; not directly outside
but further up the street, under a tree, apparently contemplat-
ing the sparrows.

'What about the back of the house?' said Owen.

'I've got a constable out there,' said Georgiades.

All the same, Owen sent Zeid round, not trusting in ordinary
constables.

Then he and Georgiades went up to the front door and rang
the bell. No one came for some time and Owen was just about
to force his way in when the door opened.

'Who—?' began a servant, but Owen pushed his way past
and went on into the mandar'ah.

A man was lying on a divan. He smelt faintly of roses.

He looked up, without surprise, when they came in.

'I know you,' he said after a moment. 'The Mamur Zapt.'

'Who did you expect?' said Owen.

The man smiled. 'Not the police at any rate,' he said.

'Hamid is taken,' said Owen.

The man shrugged.

'The Khedive will look after him,' he said.

'The Khedive *is* looking after him,' said Owen. 'Although
not, I think, in the way that you mean.'

'Really?' said the man. 'He has always looked after him before.'

'This time his luck has run out. As has yours.'

The man shrugged again.

'We will see,' he said.

'Mr. Narwat will not be available to help you this time,' said
Owen.

'No?'

'No. He might even be helping us.'

'He will not be able to help you very much.'

'But the drivers, Hussein and Ahmet, will. They will testify that you approached them at the Water Cart Depot and asked them to do something for you. Collect a bomb, from the hammam, take it in their water-cart to the Sharia Nubar Pasha, and leave it so that it would explode at the right moment to kill the Khedive.'

'It didn't work,' said the man. 'I'd always had my doubts about whether it would. It seemed too chancy.'

'Where did you get the idea from?'

'Asif.'

'And he got it from Miss Skiff. Although she didn't know how he would use it.'

The man look surprised.

'Well, yes,' he said. As a matter of fact, he did. I thought it would be rather neat. To use English learning against the English. Although, in retrospect, we could have chosen a more reliable way of doing it. It struck me at the time, as I have said, as rather chancy. But Asif was keen. He was new and eager to show he could contribute.'

'Which he wasn't later.'

'Has he been talking?'

'Yes.'

'Well, well, you do seem to have been doing the rounds.'

'I have. And I have talked to Yussef as well.'

'To Yussef? He has been taken as well? Well, I suppose he was always likely to be taken.'

'You thought Ziki might talk?'

'I thought it was more likely. Much too likely, in fact.'

'He was another like Asif, wasn't he? He didn't want to work with you any more.'

'Well, you know, people get cold feet.'

'Not Prince Hamid, though.'

He was silent for a moment. Then—

'No, not Hamid,' he said.

'Did you go back to him, or did he get back to you? When the dust had settled after the last time you tried something like this?'

'I went back to him. I was more committed. To tell the truth, I wanted to get rid of the whole Khedive family. Which would, of course, in the end have included Hamid.'

'He was just a tool?'

'A willing tool. We were both fired by the same ideals.'

'And Sayed Ali? Another tool?'

'So I hoped. But he was unreliable. In the end he backed out. I thought—people told me—that he was ga-ga. Well, so he was. But not quite ga-ga enough. Or, at least, not ga-ga all the time. He had lucid flashes. And, unfortunately, rather a sustained lucid flash at the end. I have great respect for Sayed Ali. A very astute man. As well as, of course, a devout religious leader. I think that in the end that got in the way.'

'He backed out. And with him went the chance of a broader movement behind you.'

'That would have been what I preferred. A broader movement, to thrust the Khedive from power and the British out of Egypt.'

'And you into power?'

'Oh, that would have been too much to hope for. It could perhaps have fallen to Zaghlul and the Wafd. I think, eventually, it probably *will* fall to Zaghlul and the Wafd. But I thought I would speed it along.'

'But when the movement collapsed, you had to try something else?'

'I don't like being defeated.'

'And so you decided to try and blow up the Commission?'

'Even better, in some respects, than the Khedive, don't you think? More likely to lead to the right result. The British would be bound to retaliate. Almost certainly they would over-retaliate. That would provoke Egyptians. And with luck we would get the uprising I hoped for.'

'Was it necessary to use Salah?'

'Salah? The boy? Well, why not? Think of him as a martyr. In a just cause. Do martyrs have to consciously choose martyrdom in order to count as martyrs? I don't know. It would be a good question to put to Sayed Ali.'

'I think he would probably call it murder.'

◇◇◇

One result of the attempt to blow up the Commission was that it speeded up the work of the Commission no end. Its members sensibly decided that the sooner they got out of Egypt, the better. But it had also sharpened up their thinking about political realities, and in the interval between their completing of the hearing of the evidence and their writing up of their conclusions there came surprising reports (leaked, of course, by Paul Trevelyan) that while the Commission might not go all the way in the direction Egyptians wanted, it would go quite a bit of the way. One of its likely recommendations was for complete internal independence on Egypt's part, including the right to dismiss English officials. It was that, of course, that gave rise to some discussion in the Sporting Club.

'Serve under an Egyptian? Not me!' said Carstairs, of the Sanitary Department. 'I'm off!'

And several other Carstairs felt the same.

But others wondered why not?

'Abu Gamal'—the No. 2 in the Department of Municipal Works—'has always done the work anyway,' said Blackett, the Senior Engineer in the Department. 'I think he'd be an improvement on Hambleby-Jones.'

'So how do you feel about it, Owen?' asked Zaghlul.

'Me? I've always worked under an Egyptian,' said Owen. 'The Khedive.'

'Ye-es,' said Zaghlul, 'But—'

'His Highness has particularly asked me to stay on.'

'And the British?'

'Ah, well, that's more doubtful.'

Zaghlul smiled.

'I'll put in a word for you,' he said, patting Owen on the shoulder.

◇◇◇

Zaghlul was seeing quite a lot of Owen just at the moment. Party politics had come to Egypt and Zaghlul as Leader of the Opposition, was a prominent part of the politicking. That was rather an exposed position and Zaghlul demanded official protection. Now that the Commission had left, it was judged, wrongly, that the Mamur Zapt had time on his hands so he took over responsibility for the candidates' safety. This turned out to be no less onerous than responsibility for the safety of the members of the Commission but it did build rapid bonds between protector and protected. Owen, looking ahead, thought he might be able to ride the surf.

◇◇◇

The trial of Rashid, The Man of Roses, was not long protracted. Mahmoud, who was prosecuting, had it buttoned up in no time. The chief problem was the protection of witnesses. But that was always the case in Egypt and Owen, whose responsibility it was, was used to it.

Hussein and Ahmet, who were at first inclined to deny that they had been on the planet during the period in question, were persuaded to give evidence again Rashid, and this led to some mitigation of their own sentences.

Yussef, who had never made any secret of his own misdoings anyway, cheerfully provided further evidence against Rashid. Not that it helped his own case much.

The difficult one might have been Hamid. He had always worked through other people: Rashid, and Ziki, and Asif, and, of course, Salah, and it might have been difficult to pin things on him. However, he fell ill and, sadly, died. Which was, as the Khedive told Owen, a much more reliable way of doing things.

◇◇◇

Asif served a comparatively short term in prison. While he was there he did a lot of thinking and when he was released told Miriam that much of it had been about her. He had come to the conclusion that he would leave the question of her marriage to her. She could certainly go on working at the hospital if she wished, but, after much reflection, he had decided that it should be supplemented by more education. Since it was not possible for her to follow exactly in his footsteps and go to college, he wondered if she would consider another possibility: going privately to Miss Skiff. This, in fact, turned out rather well, suiting both the intellectually hungry Miriam and the newly self-doubting Miss Skiff.

◇◇◇

Zeinab, expecting her end, at almost any moment, continued to work at the hospital. Even when the Commission reported, things remained in a state of flux in Egypt and the new Government, advisedly for a while, had more important things on its mind than Zeinab.

She was, in any case, reviewing her own future independently. Suppose that a baby came along? How much time would it take? Would she be able to continue working at the hospital? Would she be able to continue working? *Should* she, as a matter of principle, continue working?

Miriam said yes. Aisha, whom Zeinab was consulting more and more frequently these days, thought she ought to wait and see. The baby might have a view of its own, she said.

In any case, said Zeinab, the question was purely theoretical.

Owen, left out of these deliberations, as he was out of most of the weighty deliberations of the universe, continued with his work. It might not be glorious but it kept the world ticking. And that, in the Middle East, then as now, was something.

To receive a free catalog of Poisoned Pen Press titles, please contact us in one of the following ways:

Phone: 1-800-421-3976
Facsimile: 1-480-949-1707
Email: info@poisonedpenpress.com
Website: www.poisonedpenpress.com

Poisoned Pen Press
6962 E. First Ave. Ste. 103
Scottsdale, AZ 85251